A BOY IS NOT A GHOST

A BOY IS NOT A GHOST

Edeet Ravel

GROUNDWOOD BOOKS
HOUSE OF ANANSI PRESS
TORONTO / BERKELEY

Published in 2021 by Groundwood Books / House of Anansi Press
groundwoodbooks.com

Groundwood Books respectfully acknowledges that the land on which we operate is the Traditional Territory of many Nations, including the Anishinabeg, the Wendat and the Haudenosaunee. It is also the Treaty Lands of the Mississaugas of the Credit.

We gratefully acknowledge for their financial support of our publishing program the Canada Council for the Arts, the Ontario Arts Council and the Government of Canada

The author gratefully acknowledges for their generous and invaluable financial support the Canada Council for the Arts and the Ontario Arts Council.

 Canada Council Conseil des Arts
for the Arts du Canada

 ONTARIO ARTS COUNCIL
CONSEIL DES ARTS DE L'ONTARIO
an Ontario government agency
un organisme du gouvernement de l'Ontario

With the participation of the Government of Canada | Canadä
Avec la participation du gouvernement du Canada

Library and Archives Canada Cataloguing in Publication
Title: A boy is not a ghost / Edeet Ravel.
Names: Ravel, Edeet, author.
Description: Sequel to: A boy is not a bird.
Identifiers: Canadiana (print) 20200391828 | Canadiana (ebook) 20200391836 |
ISBN 9781773064987 (hardcover) | ISBN 9781773064994 (EPUB)
Classification: LCC PS8585.A8715 B693 2021 | DDC jC813/.54—dc23

Illustrations by Pam Comeau
Map by Mary Rostad
Design by Michael Solomon

Groundwood Books is a Global Certified Accessible™ (GCA by Benetech) publisher. An ebook version of this book that meets stringent accessibility standards is available to students and readers with print disabilities.

Groundwood Books is committed to protecting our natural environment. This book is made of material from well-managed FSC®-certified forests, recycled materials and other controlled sources.

Printed and bound in Canada

for
Luke, Larissa and Ivy

ONE

DRIVEN AWAY

1941

SUMMER

1

Soon to Include: Natt Silver

Exiled.

Banished.

Kicked out.

Expelled.

Driven away.

Sent packing.

I'm trying to think of all the words I know for what's happened to us. In all the languages I know. German, Russian, Ukrainian, Romanian, Yiddish, Hebrew. I don't actually know the word for "exiled" in Hebrew. I only know how to say, "Go away from here." *Lekh mi-khan.*

But German is still my first and best language, and I know at least ten ways to say "Get lost!" in German. All ten of which I have been using nonstop on the bugs that are eating me alive at the moment on this Train of Horrors.

Yes, I now live on a train.

It's been six weeks and two days since we were

forced to leave the city of Czernowitz. At this point, I feel like a world expert on what it's like to be told to get lost. Or not exactly lost, since Stalin, who is now in charge of Russia, knows exactly where we're going.

Siberia.

Area of Siberia: 13 *million* square kilometers. That's almost one-tenth of all the land on the planet!

Average temperature: I'm afraid to ask. But cold. Very, very cold.

Famous for: Being big and cold. And for being the place where they send murderers and people who rebel against the government.

Soon to include: Natt Silver.

That's me. Natt Silver, age twelve. Though I'm not a murderer or a rebel. And no one else on this train is, either.

A year and a half ago, I had a completely different life. I lived in a house with my parents in a town called Zastavna. I had a nature collection that included snake skins and driftwood that looked like Albert Einstein. I had books, a kaleidoscope, a telescope, a globe of the world. My father had two horses and a warehouse full of grain. One of his helpers had a bouncy dog named Zoomie. I went to school.

And I had a best friend with round glasses and red hair. That would be Max. Short and small, but the fastest runner you ever saw, and the best soccer player in Zastavna. Max was also very good at telling jokes and inventing stories to act out, especially the incredible adventures of the two Musketeers, Maximus and Natius.

Now I'm on an actual real-life adventure. Or that's what my mother keeps calling it. "We're having an adventure!" she exclaims every time there's a new catastrophe.

She's trying to cheer me up by looking on the bright side. You need quite a good imagination to find a bright side in our current circumstances. But my mother is up to the task.

At the moment, I'm trying to decide which part of life on Train Two, Carriage One is the worst.

Is it the fact that this is a livestock train, built for transporting cows and pigs?

Is it going to the bathroom in public, squatting over a hole in the floor?

Is it being squished with twenty-six other people in one small carriage?

(Originally we were thirty-four but eight old people have died since we boarded.)

Is it the suffocating heat that melts your brain and paralyzes your body, and only four small openings in the walls to (theoretically) let in (theoretical) air?

Is it the body lice, the flies, the mosquitoes — and the resulting welts and rashes and UNBEARABLE ITCHING all over your body, day in and day out?

Is it the water barrel that's filled with scummy

water, supposedly for drinking, and only inches away from the "toilet"?

Is it the fact that we're sleeping on narrow boards that faintly resemble bunks? Or the black loaf we get each day that faintly resembles bread? Or the bowl of rotten vegetables and warm water that doesn't even resemble soup and has the occasional worm or fish eye floating in it?

Or is it that we have no idea how much longer we'll be on this train?

Yes, that's the worst part. We have no idea when this nightmare will end. And no idea what's waiting for us once we reach our destination, wherever that is.

In the meantime, we're trapped between these four walls as the train clangs, clangs, clangs at a snail's pace.

We did have one break from train hell.

Three weeks ago we were allowed to leave our carriages and wash in a crystal lake next to one of the stations. It seems like a dream now, but it really happened.

It was bliss to cool off and wash ourselves and our clothes (we hadn't washed in over a month, so you can imagine the stench). On top of that, I ran into kids I knew from Zastavna. And, most miraculous of all, we met my old Hebrew teacher Elias and his wife, Cecilia, and their little girl, Shainie. They were supposed to be on a different train, but they managed to switch.

And then they managed to arrange another switch, from their carriage to ours.

Of course it cost money. We had to bribe the guards and also the passengers who traded places with them.

As a result of the switch, our little group has expanded. Before, it was me, my mother and Irena. Irena is a pretty eighteen-year-old teacher from our town. Her parents were sent to Siberia, but she wasn't at home when the police came for them. She was in Czernowitz, studying to be a teacher.

Irena is the only person who actually asked to join the exiles. She wants to find her parents. They could be anywhere in Siberia, but Irena is determined to track them down.

I don't know what Mama and I would have done without Irena. She's very good at taking charge. In fact, she's the representative of our carriage, along with an old man who is — or used to be — a geologist.

Now that Elias and his family have joined us, we're a group of six. Each one of us can be described by what we say most often. Which, when you're living together twenty-four hours a day with barely room to move, you get very, very used to hearing:

Mama: *Aren't we lucky to be moving away from the fighting!* (The war is taking place in Europe, and we're moving east, away from Europe.)

Irena (to the other passengers, who are always

fighting): *Stop behaving like two-year-olds!*

Elias: *Stalin certainly understands equality—we're all equally doomed.*

Cecilia: *Elias, please, I'm begging you, hold your tongue, someone will hear!*

Shainie, their cute curly-haired four-year-old: *Tell me more story, Natty!*

Me: *I'm going to literally die of itchiness!*

I've also become friends with Andreas the Tall, who was a close friend of our lawyer, Bruno the Bald. Max was the one who invented those names for Andreas and Bruno.

Bruno the Bald lived in a side section of our house, back when we had a house. He disappeared last year, as soon as the Russians arrived. No one knows where he went. Maybe Andreas knows, but he's not telling.

Finally, there's Felicia, who is very sweet and has a tiny little baby. Even though it's boiling hot in the train, her head is wrapped in a cherry-red scarf that makes her look like a genie. We've taken Felicia under our wing. So we're actually a group of eight and a baby.

I hope we'll be able to stay together. That is, I hope we have enough money to bribe the guards to let us stay together.

Money has become a matter of life and death. We

need it for the bits of food the Russian farmers sell for preposterous prices at station stops.

I haven't written to Max yet. I don't want to lie to him and I can't tell him the truth, because it isn't safe. Stalin's soldiers read all the mail, and saying anything bad about Stalin or the Soviet Union can get you sent to a Gulag prison.

That's where poor Papa is, though not because of anything he said or did. You can get sent to the Gulag just because Stalin has a quota, which means his soldiers have to send a certain number of people to prison. The soldiers don't care who they arrest, as long as they meet the quota.

If they don't meet the quota, they can get shipped off to the Gulag themselves.

But today is Max's birthday, and I really feel like writing to him.

Suddenly I have an idea.

I'm going to write in code. Max is smart. He'll understand.

2

❧

First Letter to Max

August 2, 1941
Dear Max,

Happy Birthday!

I hope by now your father has sent you and your mother and sisters tickets to join him and David in Switzerland. But in case you're still in Zastavna, I'm writing to wish you happy birthday (save me a slice of cake!) and update you on our trip to Siberia so far.

Everything is going truly splendidly. We are proud to be contributing to Comrade Stalin's vision of a better world!

After we left Zastavna, we were very thoughtfully taken to a school gym in Czernowitz, where we waited for a week. As soon as we arrived at the gym, Irena showed up and asked if she could join us. Yes, Irena the music teacher's daughter. She wants to find her parents, who left for Siberia before we did.

Guess who else showed up at the gym? Mr. Elias! Along with Cecilia and little Shainie. Only he says to call him plain Elias now that he's not our teacher.

Shainie is always asking me to tell her stories. If I run out of ideas, I can tell her about the adventures of Maximus and Natius…

Then, just as German warplanes began dropping bombs on Czernowitz, we left the gym and headed for the train station.

Minutes after we boarded the train for Siberia, bullets began to rain down on the platform and on the roof of the train. It was pretty terrifying, but thanks to the courage and wisdom of Stalin's leadership, we all survived. The soldiers on the platform were truly brave and returned fire. No one hid under the train to escape the bullets.

I've been helping Irena with her Russian and she's been teaching me geography, biology and General Information. I especially like learning about the life of insects.

Insects are quite fascinating. For example, the difference between body lice and mosquitoes is extremely interesting. They both live on human blood but are very different in the way they pierce human skin to suck out the blood. We're also learning a bit of chemistry, such as the composition of air and why we all need oxygen.

So you see our time on the train is very productive!

We are being truly well taken care of on the train. The barrel of fresh drinking water is replaced at every station, and we are given a large loaf of solid, nutritious bread and a bowl of hearty vegetable soup every day. In addition, the kind farmers of Russia sell us food on the platform at every station. The prices are reasonable and we're all eating well. I'm in much better shape than I was. As you know, I was a bit chubby before we left. Now I have a much more lean, athletic look.

Guess who else is in our train carriage? Andreas the Tall! He arrived with his mother, but unfortunately she passed away. She was very old, and though everything was done to ensure her comfort and well-being, she died. Andreas is reading The Magic Mountain. It's about people who lie under blankets in the Alps and think about life.

The train carriages are equipped with a type of very clever and convenient Barrel Toilet, but in our carriage, the Barrel Toilet was replaced with a Floor Toilet at the first stop we made, thanks to a helpful guard with a saw. The Floor Toilet is even better.

<u>Believe it or not,</u> three weeks ago we stopped at a lake. We had the time of our lives, splashing around in the cool, refreshing water!! As you know, this is a beautiful part of the world, with its crystal waters and the tall mountains in the distance, and the deep blue sky. I met some kids from school at the gym in Czernowitz and then again at the lake. They're on our train, but in different carriages. We're all a little pale from the long train ride, but as soon as we arrive at our destination, the fresh air will bring the color back to our cheeks.

Thank you again for the envelopes and pencils and paper you gave me before we left. As you see they're now coming in very handy. As are all your other precious gifts.

I'm sure the funny hat will be especially useful.

Once we're settled in our new home, I will send you an address. We are very excited about our future in Siberia, which we know will be a truly satisfying experience! If I see any Siberian tigers, I'll let you know. (If I live to tell the tale, that is.)

I will write again soon. Shainie is pestering me to tell her another story so I will sign off. Also my hand is getting tired. Regards to all.

Your brother-in-arms, Natius

3

Natt the Tiger

No-vo-si-birsk. No-vo-si-birsk.

I repeat the word over and over, trying to turn it into something ordinary instead of the name of a strange new place a million miles from home.

Our train journey is over at last. The city of Novosibirsk, Siberia, is our final stop.

Surely nothing can be worse than life on Train Two, Carriage One?

But…what if it *is* worse?

As we fold what remains of our filthy blankets, pillows and quilts, my mother tries to pretend, as usual, that everything is splendid.

"Novosibirsk!" she says happily. "What good news! It's a really big city, 400,000 people, and it's in southern Siberia!"

She's ignoring the fact that her left toe is black and blue and probably infected, one of her eyes is red and puffy, she has welts all over her body from insect bites, and she's so skinny I'd never know it was my own mother if I saw her from the back.

Irena is smiling, too. "I'm sure I'll be able to get information about my parents now," she says. "The army's Siberian headquarters are in Novosibirsk."

Then, all of a sudden, tears well up in her eyes.

I can't help being shocked. No matter how bad things were on the train, Irena always told us to rise above it. "Rise above it, rise above it," she kept saying, whenever someone wailed that they couldn't take any more.

Irena often sat with me on my top bunk, and we looked at the passing landscape through the small window opening. She'd begin with facts about what we were seeing—the Ural Mountains, types of wildflowers, phases of the moon—but she'd soon move on to volcanoes, African jungles, space rockets. She taught me about the Periodic Table and why water boils (molecules!) and how magnets work.

I think Irena literally saved me from losing my mind.

"I'm just relieved, Natt," she says, wiping her eyes. "We're here, finally. What a long train ride. It would have been faster to walk!"

There's a loud creak as the soldiers remove the door bolts, and we all pour out onto the platform.

Anyone seeing us would think we were drunk, the

way we're stumbling and losing our balance. We haven't used our leg muscles in so long, they've forgotten how to hold us up.

The station is even bigger than the one in Czernowitz, and the station building is even more like a palace.

That means we can spread out.

And right now, spreading out under the warm sun seems like the greatest luxury known to man, woman or child. I imagine a tiger feeling this way, if he was let out of his cage after years in a zoo.

That's me, Natt the Tiger.

"Natt! Over here!"

The kids who were in the other carriages have spotted me. We hug each other and make silly faces and stagger around the platform laughing. We're all a little soft in the head from being cooped up in the Train of Horrors for two months.

"Letters to friends and family may be deposited here," a guard bellows into a megaphone. He lifts a wooden mail crate and sets it on a ledge. People begin to scrounge around for paper and pens. Word gets round that there are postcards for sale inside the enormous station building.

My friends and I wobble over to the postcards, which are stacked on a long table. A soldier is in charge of selling the postcards and he's even handing out free stamps.

The message is loud and clear. The government is interested in our mail.

Some of the postcards are in color, and I wish I could buy one for Max. They're only two kopeks, but I don't have any money.

The black-and-white postcards are free. They show a photo of Stalin and Lenin sitting together on a bench. Lenin looks suspicious in the photo, as if he already knows just how bad Stalin is going to be when he takes over as leader of the Soviet Union.

I help myself to a postcard (I'm only allowed one) because paper of any kind is precious.

Back outside, everyone is writing letters and whispering, "Be careful" and "Stick to neutral facts."

In other words, don't complain about anything, if you value your life.

Felicia asks me to hold her sleeping baby while she scribbles a quick note, and then Elias hands me everyone's letters and cards and says, "Natt, you'll be our mailman."

I add my letter to Max to the pile and head for the mail crate.

The sun is still shining, but it's suppertime, and three trucks arrive with food for sale. The prices, as usual, are astronomical.

We're low on money, so we try trading with the vendor closest to us. She's a young woman with broad shoulders and a red, sweaty face.

My mother shows her an embroidered nightgown that is so fancy the red-faced woman thinks it's a party dress, and she agrees to take the gown in exchange for soft bread, four hard-boiled eggs and dried fish.

I'm pretty excited about the soft bread and the eggs. Mostly we've been living on onions, hard cheese, the occasional boiled potato, and black bread that is a close cousin to rocks.

As soon as the food vendors leave, trucks arrive for us. The journey gives me a chance to see more of the town. We're in Siberia, but Novosibirsk could be anywhere. Ordinary people wearing ordinary clothes are doing ordinary things.

I'm praying we can stay here.

The truck stops at a large wooden building that turns out to be a school, and we're led into the schoolyard.

This is where we'll be sleeping. If it rains, we're out of luck.

As we settle down, I see that the fence around the yard is nothing more than a few shoulder-high wooden poles with two horizontal logs connecting them. We're expected to climb between the logs to reach the toilet cabin.

Yes, a toilet cabin! For the first time in two months, I'll be able to go to the toilet in privacy.

Even more amazing, attached to the wall of the school is an OUTDOOR TAP WITH RUNNING

WATER! Clean, fresh water. I can't imagine anything more wonderful. We all line up to take a drink and wash our face and hands.

If this is Siberia, it's not so bad.

Our little group sets up in the yard. Everyone is in a good mood, thanks to the TAP WITH RUNNING WATER, the fresh air, the big town around us.

Even Elias smiles as he lifts Shainie up in the air.

We eat the food we bought at the station. The bread is so delicious, it brings tears to my eyes. Memories of being with Papa in Zastavna come flooding back. I think about the cheese and sauerkraut sandwiches the two of us used to eat when we rode in the cart to buy grain from farmers.

Most of the time I try not to think about my father. I try not to think about the horrible thing I did.

Papa was arrested a year ago, right after the Russians took over Zastavna. Even though he was in our town prison for the first eight months, we weren't allowed to visit. But one time, Mama got lucky. A guard secretly told her that we could walk by the prison at a certain hour, and Papa would see us through the window.

That's when I did the worst thing in the world.

As we walked by, I turned my head away.

I will never, ever forgive myself.

Two weeks after I turned my head away, on the day before my twelfth birthday, Papa had a fake trial and was sentenced to hard labor in Magadan, the farthest corner of coldest Siberia.

Now, eating the delicious soft bread, I wonder what poor Papa is eating in the Gulag. I feel tears trickling down my cheeks.

"Everyone, get ready!" a guard blares into a megaphone. "Line up in twos, women in one line, men in another. We're going to the banya."

I don't know what a banya is, but I'm glad for any distraction. If I think too much about Papa, I'll go off the deep end.

"It's only a steam bath," Elias reassures me as we begin to march down the street. I'm a bit scared because I've never been to a steam bath before, but the women and girls go into the wooden hut first, and they come out laughing.

The men and boys go next. We take off our bug-infested clothes, and clouds of steam rise from water poured on hot stones. The hot steam washes away our grime.

Best of all, the steam washes away the tiny black lice still clinging to our skin.

Russian attendants hit our backs and arms with *venik*—birch branches covered with sweet-smelling leaves. It feels strange at first. Then it starts to feel good, especially since I'm so itchy. I begin to laugh, too.

When our clothes are returned to us, they've been disinfected. The lice are really and truly gone, though we'll have to make sure they aren't hiding in our blankets.

As I fall asleep, I dream of magnificent Siberian tigers running through the forest in a heavy fog. At first the tigers can't see where they're going. But then children appear, laughing and shaking huge stalks of *venik* that magically lift the fog.

By the second day, we're all feeling healthier. Our yellow-gray skin is slowly returning to its usual color, and we no longer look like Egyptian mummies come to life. The guards bring us cabbage and bread in the morning and then again in mid-afternoon. It's black bread, but not nearly as bad as the petrified dust they gave us on the train.

Andreas the Tall told us that the guards are living on the exact same bread and cabbage. There isn't enough food even for soldiers. All of Europe is having food problems because of the war.

So here we are, steamed clean and eating bread and cabbage in a schoolyard in Novosibirsk.

I know we're not free. We can't leave. We have nowhere to go. That's why there isn't much of a fence around us.

But for the moment, our prison is invisible, and invisible things are easier to ignore.

I can go on pretending that I'm free. Free as a bird.

4

Do You Have Any Chocolate?

It's our fourth day in Novosibirsk. I'm playing Pirates and Treasures with my friends. We're hiding pretend treasures, reading pretend maps and fighting pretend duels.

I'm surveying the lay of the land from behind a fort of suitcases when I notice that the atmosphere in the courtyard has changed.

It's much quieter than usual.

A man with round glasses and wiry hair that sticks out in every direction is moving from group to group and whispering. As soon as he finishes whispering, the group goes silent. It's as if he's cast a spell on them.

I've been trying very hard not to be a boy who's afraid of his own shadow, and I'm a lot better than I used to be. But I can't shake off the wave of panic that washes over me.

Are we going to be sent to the Gulag—or somewhere even worse?

I leave my fort and casually stroll over to my mother to see what's what. But the man with the round glasses hasn't reached our little group yet.

When he finally arrives, he crouches next to Andreas the Tall and clears his throat nervously. He has news, but it isn't about us at all.

It's about the war in Europe. I want to laugh with relief.

But before he's had a chance to say more than two words, my mother completely humiliates me by trying to block my ears in front of everyone. I push her away and move over to where Elias is sitting. He never treats me like a baby.

Then an odd thing happens. I simply can't make sense of the man's words. It's as if my thoughts are flying away from the sound of his raspy voice, flying away from the things he is saying, which are things that no one could in fact be saying.

"Excuse me, I'm going for a walk," I announce.

"Good idea," Elias says, and he gives me a gentle pat on the back.

Without looking at anyone, I get up and thread my way through the crowd to the fence. I lean my elbows on a post and look out at the dirt road. I can make out a pale strip of water in the distance, and I remember Irena telling me that one of the longest rivers in the world, the Ob, flows through Novosibirsk.

The school is on a quiet road with a large field at one end. It's relaxing to look at the field.

After a few minutes, a boy and a girl cross the field in my direction. When they see me, they stop in their tracks and stare.

I wave, and they wave back. They have a short consultation and decide to come over. They must be curious about these refugees from Eastern Europe.

"Hello," I say in Russian.

"Who are you?" the boy asks. He's a little older than me, but the girl seems to be about my age. She has dancing eyes and a few freckles on her nose. Her light brown hair is braided and wound on both sides of her head like two bread buns.

"I'm Natt," I say. "I'm from Bukovina." I can tell that doesn't mean anything to them, so I add, "About 4,500 kilometers west of here. It took us two months to get here."

"Why did you come?" the boy asks.

I wish I could tell them the truth! *I was exiled because Stalin isn't the kind, friendly leader that Comrade Martha, our principal, said he was. He's a cruel tyrant. His soldiers sent my father to a Siberian labor prison for no reason at all, and we were banished from our homes along with who knows how many other innocent people.*

But I remember Max's warning before we left: *Don't trust anyone.*

"Comrade Stalin is giving us an opportunity to help build the future," I say instead.

They look disappointed.

"Do you have any chocolate?" the girl asks me.

Chocolate! I barely remember what that is.

"No, do you?"

And suddenly all three of us burst out laughing. We're having a wild fit of giggles.

When we wind down, the girl says, "I'm Olga. I want to be a ballerina." She curves her arms over her head and performs a twirl.

"You're very good," I say politely.

"I've been going to ballet school for five and a half years. My brother Peter is going to be a pilot. What about you?"

"I want to be a chemist," I say, to my own surprise. "I like molecules."

Olga's brother nods. "Me, too."

"Will you be staying here?" Olga asks.

"They haven't told us. I really hope so. I love Novosibirsk."

I've said the right thing. They both smile proudly.

"Do you know *The Nutcracker*?" Olga asks.

What luck! I do know it. When the Russians came to our town, they organized concert nights in the community hall. The concerts consisted of the people of Zastavna sitting on chairs and listening to a record playing on a gramophone. One time the record was

The Nutcracker, and in the background there was a silent film showing Russian ballet dancers.

"Yes, I do. It's by Tchaikovsky." By a miracle I remember the composer's name.

"My ballet school is putting it on for Christmas. I hope I get to be in it. There's a part for kids."

"I'm sure you'll get chosen. Do you know Beethoven's *Moonlight Sonata?*"

But as soon as the words are out of my mouth, I realize with horror that Beethoven was German! Russia is at war with Germany, and here I am praising a German composer.

I'm terrified that I'll be reported and arrested on the spot.

But Olga exclaims, "Oh, I love the *Moonlight Sonata!*" So maybe it's okay. Beethoven lived a long time ago, after all. He didn't know there was going to be a war. "It's so beautiful! My mother knows how to play it. But she isn't here now," she adds a little sadly. "If I get to be in *The Nutcracker*, she won't see me."

I'd like to ask where her mother is, but I don't want to be rude.

"My father's away, too," I say. "He's…um…working in another city."

"Where?" Peter asks, and for a moment I'm lost for an answer.

"I forget," I lie. If I say Magadan, they'll know he's in a Gulag prison. That's what Magadan is famous for. Prisoners and gold mines. Prisoners who work in gold mines.

"Our mother is in Moscow," Peter says. "She's a translator for the government. She knows a lot of languages. She sent me a steam engine."

We all fall silent. It looks like we've run out of things to say. Or things we can say. I'm worried they'll leave and I'll never see Olga again.

"If you give me your address, I'll write to you when I know where we're going," I say.

Olga looks up at her brother. He frowns like an adult, then makes up his mind. "Ulitsa Reka 17."

"Ulitsa Reka 17," I repeat — 17 River Street.

"Well, time to go," Peter says. "We have to do our chores." He takes Olga's arm and they head off.

"Good luck building the future!" they both call out, and we all laugh again.

I wish they'd stay a little longer. How lucky they are, to have a home to go to! Lucky even to have chores. I'd do anything to have chores at my own home.

Just before they turn the corner, Olga looks back at me. I wave and she does another twirl. She looks as if she's about to lift off the ground and fly.

Maybe she likes me. Why else would she turn around to see if I was still there, and then do a twirl for me?

5

The Moon Is Happy

I'm still staring after Olga and Peter, when suddenly a tall woman with a long braid and piercing blue eyes approaches me from the other side of the fence and hands me a triangular pastry.

"For Felicia Hoffman, with the baby," she says under her breath, then hurries away.

Felicia! She's in our group. What a strange coincidence.

I hide the pastry deep inside my pocket. I look around to see if anyone has noticed, but the guards are busy talking to one another. When we first arrived, they shouted their orders and kept reminding us that if we tried to escape, we'd spend the rest of our lives in prison. No one thought they were exaggerating. We know what Stalin is like by now.

But they soon realized that we're not a troublesome bunch. We do as we're told. We're polite. We always thank them for handing out black bread and whatever else is on the menu (cabbage, cabbage or cabbage). They barely shout at all now.

But they're still strict. Irena has been begging for permission to ask about her parents at the city's army headquarters. Since she's the only one among us who volunteered to come to Siberia, she thought she might have a chance.

But the guards absolutely refuse. They like Irena, and they joke and chat with her, but they won't allow her to leave even for half an hour. They're scared they'll be sent to the Gulag themselves if they bend the rules.

So I have to be careful.

I stroll over to our group and sit next to Felicia. Her baby is fast asleep in her arms.

I reach into my pocket and retrieve the pastry.

"A tall woman asked me to give this to you," I murmur.

Felicia's eyes widen with excitement, but she controls herself as she closes one hand over the pastry.

She has to work extra hard at blending in, not only because of her little baby, but because of the big, bulky cherry-red turban. No one has ever seen her without the turban, even when we stopped for a dip at the crystal lake.

Felicia breaks open the pastry. We're all watching her now, but out of the corners of our eyes, so as not to draw attention to ourselves.

Inside the pastry, instead of filling, there's a tiny

piece of paper. Felicia reads what it says and quickly tears it up. She buries the pieces in the ground.

"That letter I wrote at the station—it was to a distant cousin who lives here," she says in a low voice. "Her husband is studying at the transportation university. And she lives only three blocks from here!" Felicia continues in an even lower voice. "She's going to help me escape, so that my darling baby has a chance. She's meeting me tonight at 2:00 a.m. behind the toilet cabin. I'll be able to stay with her."

We're all thinking the same thing: You'll get caught.

But then something happens. Something that's straight out of *The One Thousand and One Nights*, with its magic lamps and secret treasures.

Felicia hands her sleeping baby to Cecilia and unpins her red turban. Very slowly, she begins to unwind the long, cherry-red scarf, which is made of pieces of silk and cotton stitched together.

I try not to stare as the last bit of scarf slides away. Underneath the turban, Felicia is nearly bald. Only a thin fuzzy layer of yellow hair covers her scalp.

"I shaved my head before we left," she explains, "so I wouldn't get hot under the scarf."

And now we find out why she never removed her scarf. She's sewn tiny pouches along the inside.

She snips off three of the pouches with nail scissors and extracts a gold wedding band, a pair of emerald earrings and a diamond ring with two rubies on either side.

"Please take this," she says, trying to hand the wedding band to Irena. "For all your help."

But Irena shakes her head. "I didn't do anything," she insists.

Felicia turns to me. "Natt, if your mama agrees, will you come with me tonight? You won't arouse suspicion, and I'll need someone to hand over the bribe once I'm gone."

Kids don't really get into trouble with the guards, even when we misbehave. But I can see that my mother is terrified.

I look at Elias, and he smiles and nods.

"Sure," I say, pretending not to be as terrified as my mother.

"Of course," Mama says.

She's pretending, too.

I spend the evening playing with my friends. We make believe that we're animals in the wild and we have to guess which animal. Then we make believe that we're Emil and his detectives and that we're on a secret mission. But that only reminds me of my own secret mission, and I'm relieved when the adults tell us it's dinnertime.

I return to our little group. For the first time since we left home, I'm not hungry. Usually I have to force myself not to wolf down whatever food is available, even if it's just black bread.

But I'm too nervous to eat.

At nine o'clock we settle down for the night. Even though it's still warm out, I'm shivering under my down quilt. I begin to think of everything that can go wrong. The guards catch Felicia, take away her baby and send her to the Gulag. Or they arrest Mama because her son tried to help someone escape...

I tell my heart to slow down, but it won't listen. I've been embarrassed all my life by how easily I get scared, but now I realize that until tonight I didn't really know what fear was.

I try to go over our plan in my mind. Not that there's much to it. We just have to walk together to the toilet cabin and then Felicia will disappear with her baby and I'll walk back alone.

That's when I have to approach the night guard, tell him that Felicia has diphtheria, and give him one of Felicia's rings.

But what if he sees Felicia disappearing before I have a chance to talk to him? What if he follows us?

Then I remember something.

The toilet cabin is extremely—and I mean *extremely*—smelly. Everyone uses the one cabin, and the toilet is nothing but a hole in the ground. Even with the buckets of sawdust and lime that we throw down the pit, the smell can knock you down on the spot.

That's why the guards never go anywhere near the cabin. There's only one guard at night, and he'll be patrolling as far away from the toilet area as possible.

I feel much better now. I even manage to doze off for a bit. I dream I'm Emil, and my detective friends are hiding all around me behind bushes and trees, ready to come to my aid. They can even strap engines to their waists and fly. If necessary, they'll sweep down from the air and whisk me away to safety.

I nearly cry out when Felicia touches my shoulder, but I stop myself just in time. My mother is curled up inside her quilt, but she's wide awake. So is everyone else in our little group. Except, of course, for Shainie, who is fast asleep beside Cecilia.

Felicia needs both her hands to hold her baby, so I take the flashlight and lead the way. We walk toward the night guard who is patrolling just outside the fence. I point to the cabin.

"We need the toilet," I say. I've never been so grateful to be good at Russian. In fact, Russian is now my second-best language after German.

The guard nods in a bored way.

So far so good.

All at once, without warning, a man appears in the dark and dashes past us.

He has the runs, and he's rushing to the toilet. A lot of us have the runs on and off. It's one of the reasons the toilet smells so bad.

The guard snickers. What luck! The running man makes our own expedition look more ordinary. We're not the only ones who need the toilet in the middle of the night.

We follow the man to the cabin. I was right about the guard staying as far away as possible from the stench, but he's still pointing his flashlight in our direction.

Fortunately, the man with the runs remains inside for a long time, and eventually the guard turns off his flashlight. I'm praying that he's lost interest in us.

I turn off my flashlight, too. There's no time to waste.

"Take good care, my angel boy," Felicia whispers in my ear. She slips the gold band and the diamond ring into my hand, and just like that she's gone. She's disappeared into the night.

A few minutes later, the man with the runs comes out of the cabin. I shine my flashlight at his feet so that he can find his way.

"Thank you, thank you," he mutters in Ukrainian. I see now that he's the father of one of the kids from back home.

Poor guy. He looks terrible.

He, too, vanishes into the darkness.

I now have to do the hardest thing I've ever done in my life.

My heart starts to pound like a herd of wild buffaloes, and I'm clutching Felicia's rings so tightly I'm afraid I might draw blood.

The worst part is that I'm shivering from head to toe. The guard can't hear my heart, but he'll see that I'm scared.

I wish I could just slip back to the yard. But it's much too risky. If I don't bribe the guard, and he notices that Felicia's gone, he'll sound the alarm and go looking for her. She'll have the entire army after her, and we'll all get into terrible trouble.

I take a deep breath. There's no choice. I'm going to have to put on an act.

I think of my mother, and how just before we were exiled, she put on a whole show for the chief of police so he wouldn't arrest her for trying to hide. I remember how she flirted and laughed as she tried to convince him that she'd merely gone to visit an old friend who needed help. It worked.

If my mother could do it, so can I. It's a matter of life and death.

And everyone is counting on me. They picked me because I'm a kid, and guards are easier on kids. And because they believe in me. I have to live up to their expectations.

So I take a few more deep breaths and pretend that Max is right there beside me and that we're on one of our musketeer adventures.

I walk up to the guard and stop, trying to look as

if I haven't a care in the world.

"Where's the woman?" he hisses.

"She's still in the cabin," I say in my best Russian. My voice is miraculously steady. "She has a high fever. I think she might be dying of diphtheria. But she wanted you to have this." I hand him the gold ring.

He examines the ring with his flashlight. He has big furry eyebrows and a nose like a twisted pickle.

Terror is ripping through me, but I enlist every muscle in my body to fight it down.

"How dare you try to bribe me!" the guard growls, but he doesn't return the ring, and he's keeping his voice down.

"Oh, I forgot. I have this, too." I hand him the diamond ring. "It's my mother's, but you can have it. It's a real diamond and real rubies."

He passes the jewels from one hand to the other, still undecided.

I begin to panic.

Barely knowing what I'm doing, I recite the first lines of a poem by a famous Russian poet. It's called "The Bronze Horseman." We had to learn it at school.

I want to show him that I'm a good Russian, and patriotic.

He stood on the lonely, wave-swept shore,
And as he gazed at the world afar,
He let his noble daydreams soar.

"Pushkin!" the guard exclaims. "How do you know Pushkin?"

"I love Russian literature," I tell him. "I'm reading *War and Peace*." Which is at least half true. I have the book, and one of these days I might try to read it.

"You're a good boy," he says. "Very well, go back to your mother. We'll say no more about it."

I quickly climb through the fence. I need to get away before he changes his mind.

Doing my best not to step on sleeping bodies, I return to our spot. When I reach my quilt, my knees buckle, and I collapse onto the ground.

My mother whispers, "Darling?"

I whisper back, "The moon is happy." It's a line from a children's rhyme she used to read to me. She'll understand.

I sink back onto my pillow. It's a pillow we brought from home, and it's in pretty bad shape by now, but my whole body is aching, and I'm grateful for every feather.

I tell myself that I can relax now. Once the guards take a bribe, they do what they've promised, so no one will tell on them. The guard will find a way to write "deceased" next to the names of Felicia and her baby.

But Felicia is the opposite of deceased. She and her baby are alive and safe at her cousin's house.

Maybe I even saved the baby's life.

Eventually I drift off into a deep and very long sleep.

It isn't until I wake up that I feel something sharp digging into me from the ground.

I check my blanket, expecting to find a pebble.

But it isn't a pebble.

It's Felicia's emerald earrings! She slipped them into my pocket, and I didn't even notice.

I think back to the words of the fortune teller who read my palm in the gym in Czernowitz, just before we left for the endless train ride.

You will survive... many will die, but not you or your parents. You will all be reunited at the end of the war.

6

Do You Speak English?

We're woken at 5:00 a.m. by the guards' favorite pastime: shouting into the megaphone.

"Gather your belongings at once," an officer bellows. "In one hour you are leaving."

"Leaving for where?" Irena sighs as she rubs her eyes. "Why can't they ever tell us?"

"They want to make our life interesting," Cecilia says, and we all laugh nervously.

"The following individuals are to step forward," the officer continues, and he lists the names of four men and a woman. One of the men is Andreas.

The color drains from Andreas's face, and for a second I wonder if he's going to faint. Being singled out usually means arrest, and arrest means the Gulag.

But he manages to stand up and, like a man who has accepted his doom, he strides bravely toward the guard.

Ten minutes later he returns with a grin that looks almost wild, he's so relieved. It's the first time I've seen him smile, in fact. Not that he's ever unfriendly, but on the train and then in the yard, he spent most of his time buried in *The Magic Mountain*.

"What a stroke of luck! I'm staying here in Novosibirsk," he announces. "I'll be working at army headquarters."

It turns out that Andreas has a degree in physics and mathematics, and the Russians need those skills for the war effort. Stalin hates university teachers and students, but now it seems they're useful after all.

Within one day, our group has shrunk from six adults and three kids to four adults and two kids. Now it's just me and Mama, Elias and Cecilia and little Shainie, and Irena. Of course, I'm happy for Andreas, and for Felicia and her baby, but I'll miss them. They were part of our team.

Andreas pokes around in his bags and pulls out a book.

"Here's a present for you, Natt. I expect big things of you. Your father would be very proud if he were here."

It gives me a pang when he says that about my father. How can Papa be proud of a boy who turned away from him?

But Andreas means it as a compliment. I'm surprised by the compliment and by the gift. I didn't think he'd really noticed me.

The book is called *Do You Speak English?* It's for learning English!

A strange shiver runs down my spine, as if the book, like Felicia's emerald earrings, is a magic omen.

We have relatives in Canada, in the city of Montreal, and we almost joined them before the war broke out. But by the time my mother agreed to go, it was too late. I memorized the letters from Canada and showed them to my friends. A city of enormous stores, beautiful "duplex" apartments, an amusement park called Belmont with a thrilling Cyclone roller coaster.

And, best of all, no wars.

Getting organized for the next leg of our journey is no easy task, and once again we thank our stars for Irena. We'd never manage without her. She hardly brought any luggage herself, and we brought way too much. How would we have carried our things without her help? We have seven suitcases and bundles, and Mama's heavy coat.

In the end, three hours pass before we leave.

"Please line up in twos," a guard with a strange singsong voice finally instructs us. "We're walking to the river, and from there you will sail north."

Did he say sail? I'm sure that's what I heard.

We're going to sail down a river! Sounds like fun.

🙣

Second Letter to Max

September 12, 1941
Dear Max,

Remember when we were Tom and Huckleberry, sailing down the Mississippi River?

Well, guess what? I actually sailed down a real river on a real raft.

After a few days in Novosibirsk, we were told we'd be heading north. Only five people were allowed to stay, and one of them was Andreas the Tall. The army needs his expertise. The rest of us walked in pairs to the Ob River. The river looked as if it was close by, but it kept getting farther away (optical illusion). In the end it took us two hours to reach the harbor.

There were hundreds of other exiles there. We all boarded three enormous barges, which are rafts with low sides. The barges were connected by cables, like ducklings following their mother. The mother duck was a powerful tugboat. Each barge also had a huge steering oar manned first by one sailor, then a second sailor. Every six hours, they switched.

We loaded our things, and then we had to carry hundreds of boxes of food and tools that the Russians were delivering to different places.

At that point it began to pour. The whole time we were in Novosibirsk sleeping outdoors, it didn't rain, but as soon as we set off, a rainstorm came crashing down. All we could do was pull our coats over our heads.

The tugboat needed wood for its steam engine. Guess who got to supply that wood? Yes, us. Every day rowboats were lowered down to the water, and we climbed into the boats, which we then rowed to the shore.

There are forests all along the river. The adults cut the wood, and we kids gathered raspberries and pine nuts, which you roast in a fire.

No one actually knew how to cut trees. Mama and Irena tried to use a two-handed saw, but they kept losing their balance and falling backwards.

The guards had nets that had been dipped in kerosene, and they put them over their hats to keep the clouds of mosquitoes away—very clever. The mosquitoes literally made the sky dark, but such are the sacrifices we must make for Mother Russia, and we were happy to do it. We looked quite funny by the time we returned to the rowboats, with our faces and hands swollen by bites.

Eventually the passengers, including Mama, became quite good at lowering and raising and rowing the boats, handling the saws and axes and protecting themselves from the mosquitoes by working fast and wearing many layers of clothes.

After a week on the barge, we did a detour on the Tom River so we could stop at the city of Tomsk, which is even bigger than Novosibirsk.

We weren't allowed to leave the barge, but we bought food from the locals, including, _believe it or not,_ a delicious warm meal of kasha with fried onions, just like Aunt Dora used to make. She'd be pleased to know her recipe has reached all the way to Siberia.

Then we continued north, up the Tom and back to the Ob River. But this time the Ob was more like an ocean than a river.

A very stormy ocean. It also got a lot colder. When it rained, the wind was like a hammer driving icy daggers of rain into my body. The wild waves made people seasick...I will spare you the details. We couldn't even see the shore half the time, but we didn't drown.

We soon had more room on the barge, because after Tomsk, around fifty families from each barge were let off every day for resettlement at different towns. We are Special Settlers, and we feel truly privileged to be part of Stalin's resettlement plan.

The one sad part for me was that Elias and Cecilia and little Shainie had to leave the barge before us. It happened so fast that we didn't have a chance to explain that we're together.

However, a guard told us where they were going, so I'll be able to write to them.

Several wood-chopping and food-gathering stops later, our turn came to leave the barge. We were loaded onto a truck and taken to our new home.

It's called Porotnikov. It's a charming little place surrounded by the beauties of nature, including many forests and a river. I know we will be happy here. You can write to me c/o the Community House, which is where we are now, waiting to find a place to rent.

We happened to arrive on movie night, and even though there's no electricity here, and we were quite worn out from puking, we watched a film powered by a generator with a handle that someone had to turn. When the person turned the handle too fast or too slow, the film went crazy and everyone laughed, even though the subject (building wells and forges) was very interesting.

I can't wait to hear from you and to find out what you've been up to.

Your fellow musketeer, Natius

8

Rock Bottom

The worst thing has happened. You think the worst thing has already happened, but then it turns out there's something even worse.

First, I thought nothing could be worse than nine weeks on the Train of Horrors, followed by being drenched to the bone by torrential rain night after night on a rocking barge while puking your guts out overboard and hoping the puke doesn't get picked up by the wind and thrown back at you...

Then I thought nothing could be worse than being eaten alive on the riverbank by clouds of mosquitoes so dense they literally blocked out the sun, while at the same time watching the guards shout insults at poor Mama and Irena as they tried to chop down a sapling. And afterwards returning to the barge with our heads twice the size they were when we left it, thanks to the fifteen billion mosquitoes who fed on us like miniature vampires...

Then I was sure that nothing, absolutely nothing,

could be worse than arriving in the middle of Siberian nowhere and being told at the Community House where we stumbled in, shivering and feverish and half-dead, that we've been exiled for *twenty years*!

Mama and I would have fainted on the spot, but Irena whispered, "They change the numbers all the time. They're just trying to scare us." I clung to her words with all the hope that ever was in this world or ever will be...

Then it seemed that nothing could be worse than looking for a place to rent and discovering that the best we can do in this miserable "collective" is a third of a kitchen in a tiny log house. The stove, which is like a house for gnomes, takes up half the room. The husband and wife who own the house sleep on the roof of the stove, five inches below the ceiling. Their six or seven kids sleep in the only other room, and the three of us have to squish on a board between the stove and the wall, with a sheet hung from the ceiling (by Irena) for privacy. This on top of attending the freezing Community House school, where I'm in a class with kids of all ages and not learning anything I didn't already know six years ago, like how to add.

Then I thought nothing could be worse, ever, than seeing Mama and Irena fetched by the Chief of the Work Brigade at six in the morning to become "productive citizens of the glorious Soviet Union" by uprooting tree stumps, which means eleven hours of digging channels under the huge roots, sliding chains through the channels, tying the chains around the stump, then pulling the chains with the other exiles. They would come home late at night, barely able to walk, their hands covered with blisters, and Mama's face streaked with tears…

Then I was positive that nothing on this Earth could be worse than winter in Siberia, with icicles forming on your eyelashes and temperatures falling so low that if you're out for more than a few seconds without enough insulation you could end up with your toes getting amputated because of frostbite. Since it was too cold to uproot trees, the exiles had to saw blocks of ice from Porotnikov's river, bring them inland and build an ice house.

Then I decided that nothing in the entire universe could be worse than feeling hungry from morning to night, even hungrier than on the train, because back then we were able to buy food at the stations. But in Porotnikov we ran out of money and things to trade. All our extra belongings—even our precious bars of soap—went on rent and food. And seeing as we had to pay 70 rubles for a cabbage, 18 rubles for a cup of milk, 125 rubles for a cup of oil, and 10 rubles for 7 potatoes, everything was gone by the middle of winter.

All we had left were Mama's wedding band and Felicia's emerald earrings, both of which we couldn't trade for enough food, so we held on to them. At that point we had to survive on the government's daily ration of a few potatoes and black bread. Enough for half a meal, not three...

At every stage it seemed like my life had reached rock bottom, and there was simply no way things could get any worse, unless my legs turned into snakes or burst into flame—events that happened regularly in my nightmares.

But I now know that none of the above circumstances were really as bad as I thought they were, because finally, after somehow surviving an entire winter in this godforsaken corner of the planet, the worst thing really has happened.

Mama's been arrested. And it's my fault.

It happened so fast. In the morning Mama was here, and by evening she was gone.

Irena came home alone, drew the curtain around our bed and placed her arm around my shoulder.

"Your mother's been tricked," she said in a low voice. "The supervisor, Valentina, told her to take home extra potatoes at the end of the day. She said it would be okay, she'd make sure no one knew. So when we finished, your mother hid five potatoes in her coat pockets. Five minutes later, Valentina had her arrested."

I was stunned. "Why? Why would anyone do that?"

Irena sighed. "Valentina probably receives a bonus for every arrest. That's my guess. But listen, the jails here aren't like other jails. They're just cabins, and the inmates work exactly the way they work here."

"When can I see her?"

I wouldn't be able to breathe until I saw Mama.

But Irena shook her head. "Poor Natt. She's been taken to Bakchar for her trial. You must be brave. Your mother will write to you in a few days, and in the meantime she said to tell you not to worry, because she's going to be fine."

I pulled myself away from Irena and ran outside. I couldn't face anyone, because I was crying so hard it felt as if my stomach was being ripped out of my body.

I ran to the tool shed and crouched between the wheelbarrows and rakes.

My father's gone and Max is gone and now my mother's gone. Even Elias is gone. I have no one and nothing.

The worst part is that it's my fault. I tried not to complain, but Mama knew I was hungry, and she kept apologizing. She was especially apologetic on my birthday, when she and Irena tried so hard to put together something special. They didn't succeed. All I had for my thirteenth birthday was potato pancakes fried in a spoonful of precious oil.

And when Mama apologized, I didn't say, *Oh, it's fine, I'm not hungry at all. In fact, I feel quite full and satisfied.*

No, I just shrugged. I shrugged like a two-year-old! It's because of those shrugs that Mama fell for Valentina's trick. She stole those potatoes for me.

I can hear Irena calling my name. She'll soon figure out that I'm in the shed, but I don't want to see her. I don't want to see anyone.

I try to stand up, and that's when I notice that I'm soaking wet. For a moment I'm confused. Have I sat in a puddle?

Then I realize what's happened.

I've wet myself!

I don't care. I don't care about anything.

9

From Boy to Ghost

I wake up in my bed, though I barely remember how I got here.

I'm alone. Irena has already left for the day. Everyone else is still asleep, and I can hear the loud snores of the owners from the top of the stove. I pull my quilt up to my eyes.

Something terrible has happened, but what?

Oh, yes, I remember now.

My mother has been arrested. Just like Papa.

My poor mama! I refuse to cry, and the effort makes my throat hurt. If I start crying now, I'll never stop.

At least she's not going to the Gulag. Irena says my mother will be in an ordinary jail. And right now she's only twenty kilometers away, in Bakchar.

Bakchar is a real town, not like Porotnikov, and everyone wants to move there. I now understand that in Siberia, the bigger the place, the better.

Really, anywhere would be better than this miserable dump, which is nothing more than a tiny collection of tiny cabins and a pitiful Community House. As for basics like electricity and soap, I may as well be living in the Stone Age.

Suddenly I remember the warning of the fortune teller who read my palm at the gym in Czernowitz.

Beware of a woman with red eyes.

I've seen Valentina, the supervisor who tricked Mama. Of course, we're starving, so she knew my mother would be easy prey. Valentina looks like a shiny wooden puppet and, now that I think about it, her eyes are a strange rusty color. The fortune teller was right!

If only I'd had a chance to say goodbye to Mama! I want to tell her I'll be all right and remind her that I'm thirteen.

I don't know how I'll face school today. I see that Irena has washed my trousers and hung them to dry by the stove. I'm too embarrassed to think about that. I quickly get dressed and hurry out of the house before the family wakes up.

I walk to the edge of the road and sit on an overturned pail. It's the middle of May and the thunderous sound of ice cracking in the river swallows up my jumbled thoughts. You wouldn't think melting ice could make such a loud sound. When I first heard it, I thought the German army had reached Siberia and was bombing us again.

But it was only frozen water starting to melt.

I feel frozen, too, but instead of thawing, I'm getting colder.

"Natt, Natt!" I look up and see Irena rushing toward me. "I have some good news," she says, catching her breath.

I don't let myself get excited. The only good news would be that my mother is being released, and I know that's not going to happen.

I wish Irena wouldn't sound so happy. It reminds me of Mama, always pretending that we're lucky no matter how bad things get.

Irena charges full speed ahead. Whenever she gets enthusiastic, she talks so fast it's hard to keep up.

"You know how I've been trying to get a job in Bakchar? Well, now that your mother is there, I went again to see Gregor, the officer who's been helping me—we've become quite friendly—and he says there's an opening for a clerk! An indoor job! We can go right away. He even knows a place we can rent."

An indoor job is the most valuable thing an adult in Siberia can have. It often means the difference between life and death. During this past winter, seven of the older exiles died because cutting trees and chopping ice in the unimaginable cold was just too much for them.

I don't know if I'll be allowed to visit Mama in Bakchar.

But one thing is certain. I'll never look away from her the way I did with Papa. Never.

Irena grabs my arm and pulls me back to the house.

"We only have a minute to pack! I've arranged a ride with a farmer, but he's leaving right away."

Fortunately—or unfortunately—there isn't much to pack. We've traded almost everything we owned.

I gather what's left of my belongings:

- my warm coat, with Felicia's emerald earrings sewn into the hem
- the furry hat Max gave me before we left and which saved my life in the winter
- my down quilt, which is so patched up and stained it looks like a map of the Indies
- a bag of clothes
- *War and Peace* and *Do You Speak English?*
- Max's going-away present of a schoolbag filled with little treasures. I'd literally rather starve than sell those treasures.

"We have to leave at once. There's been a sudden change of plans," Irena tells the woman of the house, who is now up. Her husband is out fetching wood for the stove. I'm glad we only have to deal with one grumpy person instead of two.

The wife narrows her eyes and purses her lips. We've already paid for the month, so we don't owe her anything.

"We never really had the space," she mumbles, and

suddenly I feel sorry for her with all her kids, stuck in Porotnikov. No wonder she's always in a bad mood.

She marches into the second room where her children are still sleeping and shuts the door behind her.

The farmer arrives to take us to Bakchar, and Irena and I climb into his wagon and squeeze ourselves between the logs, sacks, barrels, jars, bits of furniture and bundles of straw.

I stare at the passing trees in a daze. I'm starting to feel like a ghostly spirit, drifting from place to place. Every day I'm becoming more invisible and less solid.

Solid kids have homes. Imaginary kids have imaginary homes.

Is this what Papa felt when I turned my head away from him? That he'd become an invisible ghost? And even his own son couldn't see him?

Poor Papa! I'm sorry!

Irena gives me a hug and says, "As soon as we get to Bakchar, I'll try to see your mother, and maybe they'll let me give her a letter from you. You know you're like a brother to me, Natt. I promised your mother I'd look after you and I will."

I know Irena means well, but her words don't really land in my brain. There's nowhere for them to land. I should be relieved that I no longer have to attend that sad excuse for a school at the Porotnikov Community House, or sleep on a board in someone's kitchen, but I'm finding it hard to feel anything.

I shut my eyes and half-doze. When I open them, four hours have passed, and we're arriving at Bakchar.

Bakchar has two main roads that cross in the middle of the town. There are houses all along the roads, some of them quite big. At one point we pass a strange yard where children with big staring eyes and streaked faces seem to be sleepwalking.

"That's the orphanage," Irena whispers in my ear, and I shudder. But no, I'm not going to be feel sad. I'm not going to feel anything. I'm a ghost, remember?

The wagon stops in front of a house that's divided into two parts, each with its own door, and Irena helps me down. She talks to someone about wood and rent and the vegetable garden, and we step into our new quarters.

We have an entire room to ourselves, with our own door to the outside. There's a small stove, a bed, a cot, a table, two stools, a clothesline and a shelf.

While Irena inspects the mattress for bedbugs, I unpack my things. I line up *Do You Speak English?* and the two volumes of *War and Peace* on the table.

Then I take out Max's treasures: envelopes and pencils and a sharpener, a ball and ten jacks, my star-dust marble, a sliding number puzzle, cards and a card-game rule book, a fake Musketeer moustache, three shoelaces (there were seven, but we used the others), tiny bandage scissors, camphor and a small bottle of iodine (what's left of it). I'm wearing the socks he gave me, and we've used up the bandages, sulfa, Aspirin, cough medicine, candles, matches and soap. I don't even remember what soap looks like.

I feel a little better now. This is my room and these are my things. Maybe Irena is right and our lives will improve here.

"Thank you, Irena," I say, and I realize it's the first time I've thanked her. My mother thanked her a million times, but not me, even though she helped us carry our luggage, kept order on the train, taught me about molecules, looked after my mother all winter, never lost her temper and has now brought us both to Bakchar.

She was right to be excited, because Bakchar is a thousand times better than Porotnikov and she has an indoor job here and won't be an exhausted wreck all the time. We might even play jacks in the evening.

"Oh, you've helped me as much as I've helped you," Irena says.

I never thought of it that way. I guess we did help Irena. Instead of being alone and on her own, she has become part of our little family.

10

Dragons vs. Dinosaurs

The next day Irena goes to work at her new job.

She's taken a letter for my mother. I knew the authorities were going to read it, so I chose my words carefully:

Dear Mama, I love you and hope you are well. Please don't worry because Irena is taking great care of me. We are now living in Bakchar and it's very nice here. I will be fine and will count the days until I see you again. Your devoted son, Natt.

I go back to sleep in my cot and don't wake up until noon. Then I eat the bread Irena left for me and head out to do a bit of exploring.

It doesn't take long to walk from one end of the town to the other. I try not to walk past the orphanage.

My mother is somewhere in this town, but where? The houses are all so shabby, gray, gloomy and shut up that any one of them could be a jail.

There are trails along the main road that lead to other parts of town, but I don't follow them. I don't want to get lost.

But I also don't want to return to an empty room, so I decide to head for the beach. It seems every town in Siberia is on one river or another.

The ice is cracking here, too. It roars and booms like a mysterious beast in a cave.

Suddenly I notice a girl on the beach. She's sitting close to the trees, which is why I didn't notice her at first. She looks a little younger than me, and she has a sweet thin face, cute squinty eyes and reddish hair.

Not as red as Max's, but more red than brown.

"The river sounds like a roaring dragon," I tell her.

She smiles. She has a very friendly smile.

"My…Russia…bad," she replies. In other words, she didn't understand a word I said.

"German?" I ask her. "Ukrainian? Yiddish? Romanian?"

She nods vigorously at my last guess.

"I was just saying that the thaw sounds like a dragon's roar," I say in Romanian.

She lights up at my translation, as if she can't believe her luck.

"Would you like some cheese?" she offers, stretching out her arm.

I nod, even though I know I should probably refuse. Food is too scarce to be shared, but I'm starving.

The cheese is soft and delicious. I haven't had soft white cheese for over a year.

"My mother works at the food-processing plant," she says. "I'm Gabriella. Gabi for short. I'm eleven. What's your name?"

"Natt. I turned thirteen on April Fool's Day."

"I'll be twelve in three months," she says. "I thought dragons didn't roar."

"Dragons are imaginary," I explain. "They can do whatever we want them to do."

"No, they aren't. There are fossils and everything."

"You mean dinosaurs."

She blushes. "Oh…I get them mixed up."

"I get things mixed up, too," I say. "I always get Iceland and Greenland mixed up. And seals and dolphins."

"And jam and lamb," she says with a straight face.

Jam and lamb?

Then I catch on. "And toes and nose," I say.

"And pins and pines."

"Ghosts and werewolves."

By now I'm laughing with Gabi the way I used to laugh with Max when we were being silly. It's a good feeling, but it also makes me homesick.

"I have to get back," Gabi says, jumping up and brushing sand off her dress.

We walk part of the way together. Then she turns onto one of the trails and we say goodbye. We don't make plans to meet again. Refugees don't make those kinds of plans. Who knows where we'll be tomorrow or what we'll be allowed to do?

I'm starving again by the time Irena returns. To my surprise, she's carrying a string bag bulbing with food.

It's been a long time since I've seen that much food in one place. A jar of borscht, pickles, an entire cabbage wrapped in newspaper, dried fish, a loaf of soft bread, a tiny jar of honey, an even tinier jar of clarified butter.

I can count on one hand the number of times I've even seen butter since we were exiled, and I'd still have five fingers left over.

"Did you see Mama?" I ask as soon as she shuts the door.

"Yes. Let's eat first, and I'll tell you all about it."

I want her to tell me everything right away, but I can see she's exhausted and hungry, so I bite my tongue.

I feel a little guilty enjoying this delicious food while my mother is suffering, but Irena, who notices everything, says, "It would give Sophie great pleasure to know you were eating, Natt. It's what she wants to hear."

We eat slowly. You're not allowed to eat a ton of food all at once if you've barely been eating for months. It can actually kill you!

When we've eaten as much as we dare, Irena leans back in her chair, unpins her hair and then pulls it back into a knot.

"I attended the trial today," she says. "It could have been much worse. I think Gregor used his influence." But she doesn't sound as happy as she did yesterday, and I feel my throat getting tight again. This time with fear. "There were three women judges sitting on a kind of low stage, and they whispered among themselves for about three seconds before deciding on the verdict. Sophie will be going to a prison near Tomsk. They sentenced her to one year."

"One year…" I can't believe I won't see my mother for a whole year.

"Without Gregor's help, it might have been three…"

"Gregor must be a very kind man," I manage to say.

Irena takes my hand and squeezes it. "I've figured out the system here. It's all about favors and connections — what the Russians call patronage. Gregor likes me, so he does me favors."

What does she have to do to get favors? But I get the feeling that she likes him, too. Irena doesn't do anything she doesn't want to do.

"Now, what have you been up to?" Irena asks.

"Exploring. And learning English. SHUT THE WINDOW IF YOU PLEASE," I say in English.

And for no reason that we know, we both laugh until our stomachs hurt.

11

A Beautiful Woman

I'm dreaming about Papa and Mama. We're back in our old house playing a card game with my friend Lucy, the dentist's daughter who lived across the street from us and always smelled of lavender soap.

Then suddenly Stalin is sitting at the table, and he's cheating, but we pretend not to notice. He begins to take cards out of his sleeve — all kings and queens — and we try not to move and not to upset him. Then he throws down two Gulag cards and hands one to Papa. He's going to hand the second one either to me or Lucy or Mama. We have to decide.

I shout, "I'll go, I'll go!" and I must be shouting in my sleep, because Irena shakes my shoulder to wake me.

"Bad dream?" she asks. She's already dressed and about to leave for work.

"Yes," I mumble. The dream felt so real. But Stalin is not here. And I can't go to prison instead of Mama.

I shut my eyes and pretend to go back to sleep. I

miss Mama and Papa so much! How could they leave me like this?

It's not their fault, of course. The war took them away. That's what war does. It turns you upside down and shakes you like a pair of trousers until everything falls out of your pockets and there's nothing left— not even your family and your best friend.

We've been in Bakchar for three weeks now, and I've been spending my time learning English and helping our neighbors in exchange for food. I'm also reading *War and Peace*, finally. I continued from where our teacher, Comrade Minsky, left off, with Natasha worrying that no one will ask her to dance at her first ball.

I've been to the beach a few times, but no sign of Gabi.

Today I spent five hours pulling weeds and raking earth in our landlord's vegetable garden. It's only 4:00 p.m. but I'm hungry, for a change. All I had for lunch was onion soup and two slices of bread.

I sit at the table and begin to copy English words in the margins of *War and Peace* (Tolstoy would understand). I barely notice when the door opens.

It's Irena, back from work earlier than usual.

"Hello, Natt," she says. "I'm glad to find you at home."

I look up from my copying. I can see at once that Irena has something to tell me.

What now?

She sinks into a chair and takes a deep breath.

"Natt dear, the Soviet Union has just announced that all Polish citizens are free to go wherever they like. As you know, my father is from Poland and I speak Polish, and I visited my relatives in Lublin when I was a little girl. So they've given me permission to leave. I plan to return to Novosibirsk, and from there I'll apply for a job in Moscow. I'll have a better chance of reuniting with my parents in Moscow."

Irena pauses and presses her palms together under her chin, as if she's praying.

"Natt," she says, "I'd like you to come with me. I can say you're my brother and get papers for you, too. It would make me so happy if you agreed."

My pencil slips from my hand and rolls to the floor. I pick it up and wander over to the window. I don't want Irena to see my face, even though I don't think there's any expression on it, judging by how empty I suddenly feel.

What should I do?

I stare hard at the trees beyond the garden, as if they hold the answer.

If I go with Irena, I'll be thousands of kilometers away from Mama. She'll be alone when she comes out of prison, and who knows when I'll see her again.

On the other hand, if I don't go with Irena, I'll be

on my own. I can't even ask for permission to join Elias. I know he'd take me in, but I don't know where he is. I wrote to him from Porotnikov, but there was no answer. He was probably relocated.

If only Irena would stay! But she can't change her plans just for me. She's been trying to find her parents from the start.

A strange numbness has come over me.

"You always get what you want," I mutter.

Irena looks a little hurt, and I wish I could take back my words, but I don't apologize.

"I don't think any of us are getting what we deserve," Irena says.

"I can't come with you." My voice comes out angrier than I intend. "I have to stay for Mama."

She nods and tries to smile.

"I understand," she says. "But think it over, Natt. Either way, don't worry. If you decide to stay, I'll find a family to take you in. But we have to hurry. My pass expires in five days."

I don't answer because I have nothing to say.

Irena prepares our supper, but I can't even look at food. I decide to go for a walk. And for some reason, my feet take me to the orphanage.

The orphanage is the scariest, most pitiful place in Bakchar, and usually I try to avoid it.

The orphans are forced to work in the fields, and I've seen them marching down the road with shovels on their shoulders. Their bodies are bent forward as if they are a hundred years old, and their gray outfits look like prison uniforms. Their faces are pale, and their heads are shaven. The supervisor makes them sing songs about Russia and Stalin, but their singing sounds more like a funeral chant.

Will I end up being one of them?

I want to see them now, look into their eyes.

But when I reach the orphanage, the courtyard is empty. The children are all inside.

I find myself back in our room, though I don't remember how I got there. I don't know what I'm feeling or thinking.

Irena offers me a bowl of soup, but I shake my head and get into bed. I just want this day to be over.

In the morning we set off on a round of visits to other exiled families, asking at each house whether they'd be willing to take me in. I've turned into Oliver Twist.

"Natt's a good, healthy boy," Irena says, as if she's selling a tractor. "He's a hard worker, and he'll earn his keep. He can bring water from the river and wood from the forest. He can clean the house, do laundry, cook."

But even then, no one wants me. The problem is food. Parents are finding it hard enough to feed their own kids.

"I won't leave unless we find you a place," Irena

promises. "Or maybe you can come with me as far as Novosibirsk, and we can try finding you a home there. What about your friends, Peter and Olga?"

I've been corresponding with Olga and her brother Peter for almost a year now. I love and hate their letters. *We went skiing, we went tobogganing, we had a birthday party, we saw a funny play…*

When I write back, I make my life sound just as good. I don't exactly lie, but I don't quite stick to the facts, either.

I'd rather die than go knocking at Olga's door in my patched-up rags. *Hello, I'm a beggar whose mother is in prison. Can I come live with you?*

Besides, their father has an important job. He'd never agree.

"I can't ask them," I say, and my voice sounds mechanical even to me, as if I were half-boy, half-windup toy.

After four days, we've just about given up. Everyone knows by now that I need a home, but the message is loud and clear. We don't want you.

This entire time I've barely eaten, even though Irena has been coming home these past few days with luxury items like eggs and macaroni and even cookies. Food I'd have pounced on just a week ago. But I've lost my appetite.

Irena is trying to coax me to eat when there's a knock at the door. She jumps up to open it, and the most beautiful woman I've ever seen steps into our little room.

"I'm Iona Mindru," the beautiful woman announces. "I heard about your situation, and I think we can help. We have a sweet girl, and she's always wanted a brother. I would have come sooner, but I had to persuade my husband."

I should be relieved at this unexpected stroke of luck. I should be happy.

But I don't feel anything at all, other than a little hot.

12

A Cure for Fever

I watch as Irena packs my things. She's chatting away with beautiful Mrs. Iona Mindru, and the two of them seem to be managing just fine without my help.

It's past 7:00 p.m., but there's no rush. The sun won't be setting for another two hours.

"I have some presents for you," Irena tells me, as she carefully folds my patched and darned shirts. "I'll bring them over later this evening. Natt, dear, are you feeling all right?"

I nod and Irena hands me my down quilt. The three of us set off for my new home. I'm trailing behind, partly because of the quilt on my back, and partly because I feel as if I'm made of porridge.

As we walk with our bundles, I hear someone singing in the distance. Is that the Brahms lullaby that my mother used to sing to me when I was very little? She always changed the words according to what had happened that day. "Guten Abend, gute Nacht…Good night, good night, you played so nicely with your blocks. And how you laughed when the dog knocked them down with her tail. Sweet dreams, my little man…"

Remembering something from so long ago and so far away is making me dizzy. By the time we reach the Mindru house, I can barely stand on my feet.

I know this house. I've passed it many times. It stands out because it's made of all kinds of sections and extensions that have been added to the original cabin.

I also know who lives here. I don't know his name, but he's the director of a collective farm and he's an important man in Bakchar. He's the only person who has a racehorse *plus* two cows *plus* a hen house *plus* a sow who recently gave birth to seven piglets.

Mr. and Mrs. Mindru live in the original cabin. It's only one room, but it's huge by exile standards. There's a stove, of course, as well as a large table, two fully made beds and all sorts of astonishing extras — cooking utensils, a bathing basin, a rocking chair, a rug on the floor, a ceramic water jug, a kerosene lamp. Even a mirror.

Extras you never see in the houses of refugees, because we've all traded every last thing we had for food.

I imagine what Mama would say. "Look at this lovely place, Natt! What incredible luck!" And I suppose this one time she might be right. But my whole body seems to be drooping, and all I can think about is lying down.

"My husband and daughter will be back soon," Mrs. Mindru says apologetically. "This is your bed, Natt."

My so-called bed is three boards placed side by side and supported by six blocks. "Let's collect some straw from the barn," Mrs. Mindru suggests. So the three of us gather straw and spread it on the boards. Irena smooths out the straw as best she can and covers it with our last remaining sheet. She tucks in the sides so the straw won't spill on the floor.

"Is it okay if I lie down?" I ask no one in particular. If I don't lie down within the next three seconds, I'm going to pass out.

"Of course, of course, you poor dear," Mrs. Mindru says with a friendly laugh.

"Natt's had a very grueling few weeks," Irena says. "He hasn't been sick a single day since we left Czernowitz."

"Oh, please don't worry," kind Iona Mindru says. "I understand perfectly."

I lie down and Irena covers me with the quilt, because even though I was hot a minute ago, now I'm shivering.

It's a wonder the quilt is still in one piece. This will be my eighth place to sleep since I left Zastavna. Gym floor, theoretical bunk bed on train, outdoor yard, barge floor, community center, kitchen plank, cot...

And now hay.

"I'll be back soon," Irena says, and those are the last words I hear before I black out.

I wake up three hours later. I'm hot, my shirt is soaked in sweat, and I'm desperate for a glass of water.

Everyone is asleep. I sit up and look around me.

In Siberia, I've learned, beds are always pushed against the wall that's warmest in winter, which in this case is the wall we share with the rooms next door. Our beds are lined up against this wall. Mr. and Mrs. Mindru are at the far end, and I'm closest to the entrance. The daughter is curled up on the middle bed.

I tiptoe to the water jug and pour myself a glass of water.

I do my best to be quiet, but when I try to rearrange myself on the lumpy straw, the boards creak.

The daughter opens her eyes.

"Hello, Natt," she whispers.

It's Gabi, the girl from the beach! The girl who confused dinosaurs with dragons.

"You're shivering," she says, still whispering. "Are you cold?"

"I think I have a fever…" I tell her. "I'll be fine in the morning."

"Okay, good night!"

Normally I'd be worried and embarrassed about being a nuisance on my very first day with people who were generous enough to take me in.

But nothing is normal anymore.

And when I wake up and find that my fever hasn't gone down, and when it doesn't go down over the next three weeks, and when the town nurse, who has to be bribed to make a house visit, can't find the reason, and when a visiting doctor is also puzzled, though he assures everyone that I'm not infectious, and when Mr. and Mrs. Mindru fight about me, with Mr. Mindru saying I'm a troublemaker and that he warned his wife not to take me in, and Mrs. Mindru defending me as a "poor orphan in shock" and asking her husband to have some pity, and Mr. Mindru asking who is going to take pity on *him*—I don't care one way or another.

I lie in bed, barely eating, barely aware of what's going on around me.

At the end of the third week, Mrs. Mindru decides that desperate measures are called for.

She wakes me up in the middle of the night and leads me to a pail filled with ice water. Mr. and Mrs. Mindru both have indoor jobs at the town's food-processing factory, where there are several ice huts for food storage.

Mrs. Mindru stands me in front of the pail. I'm finding it hard to remain upright after three weeks of staying in bed and not eating, but Gabi offers me her shoulder. Her mother removes my nightshirt, leaving me only in my shorts. I don't even have enough energy to wonder what's going on.

Mrs. Mindru dips a sheet into the pail and quickly wraps it around me.

My shriek probably wakes up the entire neighborhood. Even Mr. Mindru, who doesn't budge in his bed, must only be pretending to sleep as I alternate between high-pitched squeals and helpless whimpering.

As soon as the sheet warms up, which only takes a few seconds, Mrs. Mindru dips it back in the water and wraps me again. She continues dipping and wrapping for another minute or two. When I'm literally turning blue with cold, she rubs me dry with a towel, slips my nightshirt over my head, has me remove my wet shorts, takes me back to bed and covers me with my quilt.

It seems the water cure has woken up my emotions. I begin to cry and I don't even try to stop. Gabi comes over, sits on the bed beside me and folds her skinny arms around my neck.

"Don't be sad, Natt. We love you, your parents love you, all your friends love you. I'll show you an incredible tree cave that no one knows about, and all the treasures I hid there."

She chatters on in a kind, soothing voice, trying to make me feel better.

And suddenly, I do feel better. Suddenly I want to be healthy. I don't want to feel awful anymore.

"I'm hungry," I say at last, wiping my tears.

It's 4:30 a.m. by now, and the sun is beginning to rise. Luckily, Mr. and Mrs. Mindru are deep sleepers and our voices don't wake them. Gabi jumps up to prepare a snack of cheese and a boiled egg.

For the first time in over three weeks, I have an appetite.

"I think my fever is gone," I say.

"Irena came to say goodbye but she didn't want to wake you. She brought you a notebook and some gifts in a tea tin. Would you like to see the tin?"

I nod, and Gabi brings me the tin box. Tied to the box is a sheet of paper with a hand-drawn Table of Elements on one side and a note from Irena on the other:

Here is a Periodic Table and abbreviation key for you to memorize. It's the first step to being a chemist. I wish you were coming with me but I know you'll be happy with the Mindrus. You're an independent young man with a good heart and you will always do well. I will write as soon as I have an address.

Your loving friend and teacher, Irena

It's just as well, I think, that I was asleep when Irena came to say goodbye. It would have made me too sad.

I slide the note under my pillow and open the lid of the tin box.

There's an envelope inside addressed to me.

It's from Mama!

I open the envelope, and another letter drops out, from my Aunt Dora. And right away the word "Max" catches my eye.

13

Secret Code

I read Mama's letter first.

And realize immediately that the letter is in code, like my letter to Max.

The writing is a little hard to make out at first, because it's written on a newspaper page, between the lines. But I soon get the hang of it.

Dearest beloved son,

I was so happy to receive your note. I don't have much time to write, so please forgive my hurried thoughts.

First I want you to know that the good angels have been looking out for me. After the long walk to Tomsk with 100 other prisoners, my toe trouble came back, and I also had a high fever. When we arrived, I was taken straight to the prison hospital. Only in the great Soviet Union would a mere prisoner receive such care.

Once there, I was treated by an excellent doctor, Sima Israelovna, who literally saved my life and also my toe, since thanks to her it did not have to be amputated.

When I could walk again, Sima informed the prison authorities that my skills and knowledge were essential to the hospital, and they agreed to let me work as a doctor's assistant and orderly for the duration of my sentence.

I am knitting Sima a warm sweater like the one I knit for Little Thomas when his rabbit ran away.

I'm enclosing a letter from your Aunt Dora that made its way from Czernowitz to Porotnikov, then to Bakchar, and finally to Tomsk, where it found me at last. This miracle is thanks to the best postal service in the entire world and further evidence of the revolutionary wonders of this great land.

Now, my dear son, please pay close attention.

First, remain strong and healthy for the days ahead, be ready to do whatever is asked of you and make all necessary sacrifices for our Motherland.

Second, always save for a rainy day!

Third, remember that you can achieve anything you want if you just put your mind to it. Be brave and do your duty, for like a buried treasure in a garden, a great reward awaits those who are brave.

Remember that when you write to Dora, the letter is to be addressed only to Dr. Paul in Apt. 10, and please keep in mind that our enemy, the German army, is now occupying Czernowitz. You are a smart boy.

I will write again as soon as I can but I might be too busy to write often.

Your loving mother who misses you with all her heart.

The letter is about escaping from Siberia. Mama is trying to let me know that she has a secret plan.

These are the clues:

Little Thomas, when his rabbit ran away

There is no one called Little Thomas in Zastavna, but Mama often called me her little rabbit—*Mein kleiner Hase*. Mama is telling me that we too will run away.

pay close attention

Pay attention to the clues in the letter.

make all necessary sacrifices for our Motherland

She and I will have to take risks, and it might not be easy. Our Motherland refers to the two of us: Mama and me.

save for a rainy day

Hold on to Felicia's emerald earrings. We will need them. Mama's wedding band was sewn into her coat, but she probably had to use it as a bribe when she asked for permission to work at the hospital.

like a buried treasure in a garden

This is the biggest clue of all. When the Russians first came to Zastavna, before they took over our house and turned it into a bank, we buried some gold coins and dollar bills in the yard. That is the great reward. Going home, and maybe even using that money to join our relatives in Canada.

As for the rest of the letter, I'm very relieved that

Mama has an indoor job and is friends with one of the doctors.

But I'm shocked that my poor Mama had to walk all the way to Tomsk! Tomsk is 250 kilometers away. It must have taken many weeks to get there by foot. No wonder she arrived at the prison more dead than alive.

My eyes fill with tears at the thought of Mama's dreadful walk, but one thing in her letter makes me feel a little better about her arrest. My mother was one of a hundred prisoners, all from around here.

My mother was tricked because the supervisor wanted a bonus, or maybe had a quota to fill.

Quotas are the scariest part of Stalin's Russia. They're the minimum number you need to have of something—whether it's chopped trees, or the amount of cheese a factory makes, or the number of prisoners you need to arrest. If you don't meet your quota, you go to jail or to the Gulag.

If Mama was tricked, thousands of other people are being tricked, too. Or else they're being arrested for no reason at all. Or because someone didn't like them, or wanted their wheelbarrow, and so made up a lie about them. All it takes is to be suspected of not supporting Stalin "in your heart."

I'm not alone. There are kids like me everywhere, with both parents in prison and nowhere to go.

I guess that's why the orphanages are so crowded.

14

❧

Chore Boy

It's been three weeks since I read Aunt Dora's letter, and I still haven't written to Max.

Yes, the amazing news is that Max is safe!

Aunt Dora is no longer in Zastavna. She now lives with my Aunt Clara in Czernowitz.

She wrote:

My dear Sophie,
I was extremely happy to hear that you arrived in Siberia safely and that you and dear Natt have found a good place to stay. We are all well. We are now living with Clara, and the girls have become great friends with Hugo and Suzy. Letters should be addressed not to us, but to Dr. Ernest Paul, Apt. 10, as we are often away and he has very kindly agreed to collect our mail.

I have news for Natt about Max. The very day that you left, the family received their long-awaited tickets and they left that evening, taking very little with them. I was in charge of selling their belongings. Natt can write

*to Max at Poste Restante, Basel, Switzerland. I left the
address with the Zastavna post office and asked them to
redirect letters from Natt to Switzerland.*

I think of you always.

All my love, Dora

Max is in Switzerland! He made it.

The reason I haven't written to Max since I moved
to Bakchar is that I've been unbelievably busy. I
decided, when my fever was gone, not to return to
school. I want to earn my keep by helping the Mindrus. After all, Mrs. Mindru took me in, she's feeding
me, and she probably saved my life with the ice cure.
I want to repay her for coming to my rescue.

And if I don't make myself useful, Mr. Mindru
will hate me even more than he already does.

I have therefore become the official chore boy of
the household.

My chores:

1. Fetch two pails of water from the river each
morning (two trips). It's easy now that it's summer
but in winter I'm going to have to chop through
ice to get to the water. Even when it's so cold your
eyeballs hurt!

2. Chop wood for cooking. I'm getting lessons
in using an ax and saw from the the owner's father
next door. He has a Rip Van Winkle beard and
he told me to call him Dedushka, which means

Grandfather. Dedushka is old but incredibly strong and incredibly nice. I wish I could spend the whole day just following him around and doing whatever he's doing.

3. Sweep the floor daily and wash it twice a week. We walk indoors with our boots, so the boards get caked with dry mud.

4. Do the laundry once a week. I have to make extra trips to the river for water, soak the clothes for an hour, then scrub them on a stone (the invention of soap flakes seems not to have reached Siberia) and hang or spread them to dry in the sun. Even in winter people here hang laundry outside, where the clothes freeze solid in two minutes flat. They stay frozen on the clothesline overnight and then thaw indoors.

5. Tend the garden and grow potatoes. A garden needs hours of work every day. Dedushka helps me.

6. Cook potato or cabbage soup with flour and fried onions (take off fire before they turn black!), and carrots if available.

7. Stand in line at the store to buy bread and oil with our ration cards (Gabi keeps me company if I go after school hours). The cards say we're allowed to buy sugar, flour, milk, eggs, butter, sausages…but that is only the government's idea of a joke. The store never has any of those things. Sometimes they don't even have oil.

By the time the day is over, I'm so exhausted, all I can think of is crawling into my bed.

But today Mrs. Mindru is at home with a headache, and she told me to take the day off. So I grabbed a pen and paper and headed straight for Gabi's secret cave.

Gabi's cave is a kind of tent made by fallen trees that just stayed where they were and got woven together like a net. You feel all safe and cozy inside the tree-cave. Gabi uses this hideaway to store odds and ends she scavenges. She picked up an old dusty jar and cleaned it in the river, and she keeps her smallest treasures inside the jar: pebbles with unusual shapes or colors, pieces of amber or green glass polished by the water, a brass button with a broken loop, bits of a fountain pen, half a clothespin—that sort of thing. She keeps the bigger things inside a crate. Some of them remind me of my old nature collection: dried honeycomb, abandoned nests, bird eggshells.

She also has an impressive bone collection.

So that's where I am now, sitting among the bones, hidden away from the world. A perfect place to write to Max.

I still have to be careful what I write, but I'm not as worried as I was before. The reason I'm not as worried is that like Irena, I now have a "connection."

Mrs. Mindru is friendly with a captain in the NKVD!

The NKVD are the secret police who obey and carry out Stalin's orders. They also spy for him. Everyone is petrified of the NKVD. They check the quotas and they have the power to arrest you any time of the day or night.

I never imagined an NKVD officer could be friends with an exile, but I was wrong.

That's the reason Mr. and Mrs. Mindru have indoor jobs. The NKVD captain arranged it. Mr. Mindru is an accountant at the food-processing factory, and he's the one who has to write down whether or not the factory is meeting its quota.

When the managers steal food, which happens every day, Mr. Mindru has to change the numbers to make it look as if they're still meeting the quota. The managers bribe him with cheese, milk and eggs, which he brings home in his satchel. That's the reason the Mindrus were able to take me in.

Mr. Mindru has to accept the bribes. Otherwise the managers will think he isn't on their side. On the other hand, if he gets caught, he'll be instantly shipped off to the Gulag.

No wonder he's always in a bad mood.

I think he's also jealous that his beautiful wife is friends with the NKVD captain. Gabi goes along whenever her mother visits the captain, and that's how Gabi became friends with the captain's son, Igor.

Igor is sixteen, but he doesn't mind that Gabi and

I are a lot younger than him. Igor is the second-most fun boy I've known, after Max.

I got into big trouble because of Igor, but it was worth it.

15

Third Letter to Max

August 4, 1942
Hello, comrade in arms!

Word has reached me that my fellow musketeer is garrisoned in the Citadel of Basel, and I send this missive to you with hearty greetings!

Seriously, Max, it was good to find out (from Dora) that you're in Switzerland. I can't wait to hear from you. I'm missing your birthday for the second time in a row. Many happy returns. I hope it was more interesting than mine. We were too busy to celebrate. But I must say, I like being thirteen.

I have a lot of news, too much for one letter, so I'll only give you the highlights.

I now live in a town called Bakchar, with Mr. and Mrs. Mindru and their daughter Gabi. (My mother had to leave for Tomsk.) You'd like Gabi. She's clever and good-natured and has a fantastic bone collection. The Mindrus rent part of a bigger house and I'm also friends with the landlord's father, who is old but as strong as a bear. I call him Dedushka and he really does act as if he's my grandfather. You'd love his stories. They're hilarious. Like how he dressed up his goat in his sister's clothes, taught the goat to dance, and then convinced all his friends that a witch had turned his sister into a goat...

My third friend is Igor, who is sixteen. He's the son of a captain in the NKVD. *He's fantastic with machines and knows how everything works. He's been operating the town's movie projector since he was twelve, when the regular projectionist was drafted into the army. Sometimes he invites me to come to the projection room on movie nights, and I watch the movie for free (otherwise I'd have to pay four rubles, which I don't have) through the opening in the wall. Most of the movies are from Hollywood. They made it all the way to Siberia, right in the middle of a war!!*

I've seen Stagecoach, Juarez, The Life of Emile Zola *and* The Great Waltz. *I love Bette Davis and John Wayne and all the dancing and singing in* The Great Waltz. *I love movies! Do you get to see any in Switzerland?*

Apart from my three friends, Mrs. Mindru is also really nice to me. My only problem is Mr. Mindru. He hated the whole idea of taking me in, and he hates me more every day. Just looking at me puts him in a rage.

As a result, I don't go to school. I just do chores all day. Dedushka helps me. I don't know what I'd do without him.

My hardest chore is filling the banya barrel. A banya

is a type of steam bath. They took us to a big one in No-vosibirsk so we could get clean after the long train ride. From the outside it looks like an ordinary cabin, but it's actually an ingenious invention.

First you walk into an unheated entrance room and strip, even if it's 40 below zero! If you're lucky, a bit of heat from the main room trickles in. Either way, you have to strip at the speed of lightning.

Then you go into the main room, which has a huge wooden barrel filled with water and a big pile of large stones that are heated by a stove. The stones get so hot that when you pour water on them, the whole place fills up with steam.

Then to get clean and get the blood flowing, you hit yourself with birch branches covered with leaves, which kind of hurts and kind of feels good. It gets so hot you can hardly breathe. Even though we don't have soap, you come out of it as clean as you've ever been in your life.

In summer you need the banya to get rid of all the grime from planting, cutting trees, etc., and in winter you need it so as not to lose your mind from all the cold.

We're lucky because our landlord has his own small banya, and we're allowed to use it every two or three weeks as long as I bring the water for the stones. That takes around four hours of carrying pails from the river. Then you have to wait two hours for the stones to heat up. But it's definitely worth it. I go after everyone else is finished, but there's always enough steam left. I like being alone in there. For a little while, I can be Natius again…

I'm running out of paper so I'll just tell you about how I got into huge trouble.

It was because of Igor. Another thing Igor is really good at, apart from machines, is nature. He knows everything there is to know about the forest, the river, campfires, everything. He even likes to sleep outside in summer.

So when he invited me to spend the day swimming and having a picnic, I said yes. I'd already brought two pails of water to the house, and I didn't have to make supper because we were having cheese, and I figured everything else could wait.

<u>*Believe it or not,*</u> *I had my first fun day since we left Zastavna. First we went swimming, which means dashing into the freezing cold water and hopping in the water for around ten minutes before your teeth start to chatter. It's a riot.*

Then we made a campfire and stuck two potatoes into the coals. Igor told me that the flies can get so bad in some parts of Siberia that that they can actually put out a campfire just by falling down on it in swarms!

Then he showed me how not to get lost in the woods. He has a real compass that belongs to his father, and he explained how it works. We gathered berries and saw a white eagle-owl with fearsome orange eyes, four ears and black streaks. We climbed a really high tree and Igor taught me a very rude song and then we acted out Stagecoach.

When I got home it was pretty late. I lost track of time because the sun sets so late, and I didn't think anyone would miss me.

But Mr. Mindru exploded.

Mrs. Mindru and Gabi weren't home. It was just him. He slapped my face. Then he pulled my ear and pushed me down to the floor to show me how dirty it was because I didn't sweep, and he pointed out all the other things I hadn't done and called me an ungrateful good-for-nothing lazy scoundrel. Then he slapped my behind and kicked me out of the house.

I climbed the ladder to the space under the roof of the house where the banya branches are kept. You can only get to that attic space from outside. I covered myself with the leaves and had a good cry, even though musketeers don't cry.

My parents would never have let anyone be so horrible to me. Neither would Irena or Elias or Andreas the Tall. But I was as good as an orphan.

In short, I felt nice and sorry for myself.

But an hour later Gabi came home, and I heard her calling my name. I called back and she climbed up the ladder and gave me a piece of bread. She said not to worry because her mother would never allow me to sleep in the attic.

And she was right. Mrs. Mindru told us both to come down and she even had a treat for me, a kind of liquid cheese. It's one of the best things I've ever tasted in my life.

Thankfully, Mr. Mindru was already in bed, pretending to be asleep.

Please give my best regards to your parents and sisters and to David. Have you heard from Michael? Has he sent you any more drawings? Please tell me what Basel is like and whether you get to eat Swiss chocolate. I dream of chocolate at night. Big heaps of chocolate cream pie. Even though I'm happy to make sacrifices for the great Soviet Union.

All for one and one for all!
Your friend, Natius

TWO
SECRET PLANS

1942
FALL

1

Good Manners Come in Handy

Gabi and I run home after standing in line for bread and then hurry to the stove to thaw out. It's November, and in Siberia that means winter has arrived in all its glory, and it's cold. Very cold.

"There's a letter for you," Mr. Mindru growls, as if the letter is a big bother that I've introduced into his life. But I'm used to him by now.

The letter must be from my mother, or maybe even from Max. It's been five months since my mother sent her coded letter, and I haven't heard from her since. Mrs. Mindru told me that prisoners aren't allowed to write very often, and not to worry.

But the letter isn't from Max, and it isn't from my mother.

It's from Sima Israelovna, the doctor my mother works for at the prison. And the odd thing is that it's addressed not to Natt Silver, but to Natt *Sokolov*, c/o the Mindrus.

Did she get my last name wrong? The Mindrus probably don't remember my last name, since here I'm only Natt, or the Russian version, Natan.

I sit on my straw bed and tear open the envelope.

Dear Natt, I am a friend of your mother, who has knitted many lovely things for me, and she has told me what a clever and serious boy you are and how proud she is of you. I am writing to let you know that when your travel pass comes through, you must come stay with me at Tomsk. Don't forget to make sure that Sokolov is spelled correctly on the pass. Your father will at some point be getting some leave from the Russian army and will very much want to see you. There is no rush however. I look forward to meeting you in person.

Your comrade, Sima Israelovna, Member of the CPSU

I study the letter. It's in code, as usual, and I want to make sure I decipher it correctly. She's giving me my next set of instructions.

1. I must tell everyone that my last name is Sokolov.
2. I must get a travel pass for Tomsk in the name of Sokolov.

3. I must pretend I have a father in the Russian army who is getting leave and that I need to go to Tomsk to meet him.
4. I must not tell anyone that my mother is in jail.
5. I must be clever and careful.

How in the world am I to get a travel pass?

But no sooner have I asked the question, than an answer presents itself. My friend Igor is not only great at machines and at making campfires in the woods. He's also the son of a captain in the NKVD, the all-powerful secret police.

Maybe I can get a travel pass through Igor's mother, who can ask her husband for me.

I've been to Igor's house a few times now, and though I've never met his father, his mother loves what she calls my European manners. I don't give a little bow, since Comrade Martha, our teacher in Zastavna, told us that socialists don't bow, and I don't want to get into trouble.

But I do everything else my parents taught me. I hold the chair for her when she's about to sit, I hold her coat when she's going out, I open the door for her, I use a knife and fork the way you're supposed to, I excuse myself when I leave the room, I beg her pardon if I make a mistake. I compliment her on her appearance and her cooking. I thank her for her hospitality.

I don't often have a chance to practice my manners,

so when I visit someone important like Igor's mother, I grab the opportunity. Being polite helps me hold on to who I was before we were exiled. It makes me feel less like a ghost. Here in Siberia no one does any of those things, and I could easily forget everything my parents taught me.

People also swear here. Every second word is a bad word. But my parents don't like swearing, and I want to be the boy they knew, so that when we meet again, they won't think I'm someone else, someone different.

After a visit, Igor has a blast imitating me. He laughs so hard tears roll down his cheeks, and I join in. *Oh, Madam, let me hold that chair for you in case you've had a stroke and can't do it yourself,* he says in a hilarious voice.

I can see how peculiar it all looks from his point of view, but I go on doing what comes naturally to me, and I think he invites me to his house just to have another chance to laugh hysterically afterwards.

Igor's mother also finds it funny, but she thinks I'm "adorable."

"You're straight out of pre-Revolutionary St. Petersburg," she says.

At first I was very nervous visiting the house of a captain in the NKVD. But Igor's father works long hours, and I've never even seen him. I'd probably freeze with terror if I did.

Now it seems as if my European manners might help me get to Tomsk. All I have to do is ask Igor whether his mother can arrange a travel pass for me through her husband.

Suddenly I feel hopeful. I was right. My mother is hatching an escape plan.

Good thing I didn't go with Irena! I still haven't heard from her. I hope she's okay.

I put the letter away and help Gabi slice the bread. I pretend that everything is exactly the same, even though the whole world has changed for me. I'm excited and also scared.

Will I be brave enough?

Will I succeed in this mission?

Escaping from Siberia is far harder than helping Felicia with the guard, which took only a few minutes. This mission will take weeks and months.

Mrs. Mindru comes home and we sit down to eat. She praises my soup and asks Gabi about her day. It's hard for me to concentrate but I do my best.

From now on, a part of me will be hidden from everyone, even from Gabi. There will be outside Natt, and secret Natt.

I also have to practice not calling attention to myself, so that when I do slip away, no one will notice, like Felicia when she stepped into the dark. I have to practice being a ghost again.

When it's time for bed, I can't calm down. I always

fall asleep immediately, because I work so hard during the day. But tonight my body is restless, and phrases from *Do You Speak English?* dance through my dreams all night, like magic chants.

come here
leave me
come back quickly
goodbye
stay
open the door
shut the window
I know nothing
what have you done?
answer me
help me
I am weary
whither will we go?

2

Gabi

I've decided to tell Gabi everything.

I trust her. I know she won't tell anyone if I swear her to secrecy. She's not a blabbermouth.

"Can you leave school early today?" I whisper to her in the morning. "I need to speak with you in private."

So Gabi tells her teacher that she has an earache and leaves school an hour early. Her parents are still at work, and we have the house to ourselves, but we keep our voices low, in case someone can hear us through the walls.

We sit at the table and drink white tea — that is, plain boiled water. I look at Gabi's slender fingers curled around the warm glass, and I suddenly feel sad.

I'm going to miss her.

Even worse, she's going to miss me.

"Can I tell you a secret?" I begin. "Just between us?"

Gabi nods, but she looks worried. Maybe she's guessed what the secret is.

"And we can't talk about it if anyone's around, especially Igor—"

"Don't worry. I won't tell a soul."

"My mother has a plan for us to leave Siberia, and she sent me instructions. Have you ever mentioned to Igor that my parents are in prison?"

Gabi's raises her eyebrows, which makes her cute squinty eyes even squintier. "Oh, no! He just thinks you're staying with us because you're my cousin."

Gabi and I don't know why Igor thought we were cousins. Maybe that's what Mrs. Mindru told his father. When I first went over to Igor's house, he introduced me to his mother as "Natt Mindru."

"That's good," I continue. "Because I need to get a travel pass to Tomsk, and I'm thinking of asking Igor if his mother might agree to help me."

"Oh, I'm sure she will! She loves you…" Gabi says, giggling. I smile. We're both remembering Igor's hilarious imitations of my European manners.

"And then I have to find someone to take me. And I'll need to save dried bread for the journey, because I haven't a kopek to my name."

"We could hang the bread in the storage space under the roof, in a potato sack."

I feel so much better now that I've shared my secret. "Thank you, Gabi. Oh, by the way, my new name is Natt Sokolov."

"Not Silver?"

She remembered my last name!

"It seems I've had a name change."

"We can say you're my cousin, but on my mother's side."

I sigh. Stalin forces us all to be such good story-tellers. It would be fun if it were a game, but it's not fun when you're doing it because you're scared out of your wits.

"And my father is in the Russian army, fighting Hitler."

"I'm glad you told me about your plan," Gabi says, staring down at the table. "I'm really happy for you, even though I'll miss you."

I can see that she's trying hard not to show how sad she feels. I'm her only friend, really, apart from Igor, and he might not even want to be friends with her once I'm gone.

Gabi reads my mind. "I'm starting to make friends at school," she says, looking away.

3

Songs from the Past

I'm out back chopping wood and humming to myself.

We have loudspeakers in Bakchar that mostly broadcast slogans and praise for the great Soviet Union. But sometimes they take a break from politics and play music.

That music is like light warming up my soul. Russian folk songs, dance music, operettas by composers I've come to know: Kálmán, Lehár, Strauss…

Even on very cold days, when the music comes on outside, I keep walking back and forth on the snow path instead of going inside. Some of the pieces I recognize from when my parents took me to concerts in Czernowitz or from our radio at home. We also listened to records on Aunt Dora's gramophone. But a lot of the music I've never heard before.

Now I'm humming "The Blue Danube" as I bring the ax down on the logs. Chopping wood warms me up because it's hard work, though I still have to be careful not to get frostbite, and if my fingers and toes begin to hurt, I stop and go inside for a few minutes.

Suddenly I hear my name. "Natt! Hello there!"

It's Mr. Wilmer, my father's friend from Czernowitz.

I recognized Mr. Wilmer one day in early September, when I was running an errand for Dedushka. I was so excited to see him that I called out his name without thinking.

"Mr. Wilmer! Mr. Wilmer!"

Normally I'd be too shy to call out to someone, and besides, it's not the sort of thing you do in Stalin's Siberia. It's better not to draw attention to yourself or anyone else, in case an official with a quota is just waiting to pounce.

But seeing a friend of my father's stirred up a hundred different emotions. Or maybe only two or three emotions, but it felt like a hundred.

Mr. Wilmer and his two brothers owned a fleet of trucks in Czernowitz. They were also mechanics. If the truck they were driving broke down on the road, they had to know how to fix it. Mr. Wilmer transported my father's grain and drank coffee with him in Czernowitz, in the fancy Café de l'Europe on Herrengasse.

And here he was in Bakchar, a tiny town thousands of kilometers from home. What were the odds?

Mr. Wilmer didn't mind that I called out to him.

"Natt! What a coincidence!" he said, and he came over and shook my hand.

He told me that here in Bakchar he does the same thing he did back in Czernowitz. He transports goods for the government and fixes army vehicles. He's better off than most exiles, because the army really needs him. All the local mechanics are fighting the Nazis.

Mr. Wilmer doesn't have a wife or children, which means he doesn't have to worry about how to feed his family. A week after we met, he gave me a scarf and warm mitts for the winter. And whenever he comes back from one of his trips, he brings me a special treat, like canned food or macaroni, which I share with Gabi.

He waves at me now, and I'm expecting another gift, but this time he only has a message, and I'm ashamed that the first thing I thought of when I saw him was food.

Mr. Wilmer stomps his feet as he speaks. You don't really want to stand still when it's minus 15.

"Hello, Natt. Mr. Goldman would like you to visit him tomorrow at around two in the afternoon, if you can. No need to tell anyone."

"Do you know—"

But he's already dashing back to his truck. "I can't be there myself. I have to make a delivery," he calls out, just before shutting the driver's door.

I'm very curious about this mysterious invitation, especially since I barely know Mr. Goldman. He was one of the people who refused to take me in when Irena left.

The next day I make my way to his log cabin. The place is packed with people when I arrive, all squished in one room. It reminds me of the day we found out the Russians were taking over our town, and everyone came to our house in Zastavna because we had a radio. They were all crowded together in my parents' bedroom, very quiet and still, trying to catch every word the radio announcer said.

It feels like a million years ago.

"We're here to celebrate the victory of the Red Army over the Germans in Stalingrad," Mr. Goldman announces.

I understand. He's giving us all an alibi. The Red Army victory is the story we'll be sticking to if anyone asks.

A woman moves aside so I can get through. On a table in the middle of the room there are eight tiny potatoes lined up in a row, and a ninth one on a piece of wood. Each potato has a little hole filled with oil and a piece of string that's meant to be a wick.

I haven't thought about the holidays in so long that it actually takes me a few seconds to realize that I'm at a Hanukkah party. Not that I've been able to forget I'm Jewish in Siberia. It seems that no matter where you go, there are always people who don't like Jews. I've had my share of insults from other kids and even some adults. I just pretend I'm in a play and that the people insulting me are actors saying their lines.

But I haven't done any of the things we used to do at home since we left, like celebrate holidays and light candles on Friday night. We weren't religious, but my mother liked to keep the traditions.

I know I should leave immediately. Stalin doesn't allow religious ceremonies, and we could all get into trouble. It would destroy my plans completely if I was caught. Why is Mr. Goldman putting me in danger? Did Mr. Wilmer know what the invitation was for when he gave me the message?

But maybe it's okay. After all, I'm just a boy. Boys don't get sent to the Gulag. And Mr. Goldman doesn't know that I have a plan. Neither does Mr. Wilmer.

We softly sing two Hanukkah songs. The songs stir up a whole ocean of memories. Like playing dreidel with Max. Or stuffing myself senseless with potato latkes and trying to decide whether latkes were best with jam, sour cream, plain sugar or maybe all three ...

"On this holiday, we celebrate the defeat of the powerful enemy by a miracle," Mr. Goldman says.

We each get a latke, and there are dreidels made of newspaper for the kids. I stick one in my pocket for Gabi. The Mindrus are Jewish, but they don't celebrate holidays or follow any other traditions. I'm sure Gabi has never seen a dreidel.

After about half an hour we leave. It's too risky to stay any longer.

I almost wish I hadn't gone. I don't want to think about the past now. It makes me too sad.

But now other Hanukkah songs come back to me, and I remember how much fun we had at our Hanukkah quiz parties with Mr. Elias.

I hope they're all safe—Elias, Cecilia and little Shainie. I hope someone is telling Shainie stories.

It's very cold out, but I'm not in a hurry to get home. I decide that remembering is both the best thing and the worst thing, but that you have to remember.

If you don't remember, you really are a ghost.

4

Baba Yaga Could Snatch You Away

I'm shoveling snow, for a change, when Igor shows up with an old pair of skis for me. You tie them to your boots with a cord that goes through a slot in the skis.

I don't care that I can barely lift my feet and that the skis keep twisting in the wrong direction. We have a lot of fun falling and getting up and pretending we're actually skiing.

When our fingers and toes begin to send us sos signals, Igor invites me over for warm milk.

What luck! I decide to take the plunge and ask about the travel pass. My heart begins to pound in my chest. I wish my heart would take a hold of itself now and then.

Igor's house is as big as the one our landlord and Dedushka live in. His younger brother and sister, who are seven and nine, are home, but his mother has gone out. I still haven't seen his NKVD father.

We sit at the polished table and Igor pours me half a cup of warm milk. Igor's brother and sister keep begging Igor to get them cookies from a tall shelf they can't reach, and he keeps telling them to behave.

"If you don't behave, Baba Yaga will come at night and snatch you away," he teases. Baba Yaga is a scary witch in Russian fairy tales. She flies through the air in a big mortar bowl, looking for children to eat.

"No, she won't!" Igor's sister shouts. But they both run upstairs and slam their bedroom door shut.

I know the feeling. You can be scared of things even when your brain tells you they're not real.

Right now I'm scared of something that is all too real. I'm scared Igor will tell me he can't help me. Or even worse—what if he sees my request as anti-Soviet and reports me to his father?

No, Igor would never do that.

In any case, I have no choice.

"I was wondering, Igor." I try to sound as if I've just this minute thought of asking him. "Would your mother be able to get me a travel pass for Tomsk? Because, you see, my father was in the Russian army fighting Hitler, but he's been wounded, and he's recovering in Tomsk. I really want to join him. He needs me."

I feel terrible lying to Igor after everything he's done for me. All summer long he took me hiking and raspberry-picking. He's told me hilarious jokes and explained how instruments like telescopes and thermometers work. He arranged for us to go on a boat. He even made me a special mosquito hat with a net, a *nakomarnik*, like the ones the guards wore when we were on the barge and had to go chop wood.

Thanks to him, I've seen eight Hollywood movies for free.

And just today he brought over the skis…

But Igor smiles and shakes his head at my long speech. He couldn't care less what my father does or who he is, or really about anything that doesn't have to do with machines or the outdoors.

"Sure," he says. "My mother loves you. She'll get you the pass, not a problem. She'll ask my father."

I want to hoot with relief. The first task has been completed. And it was so easy!

Igor, I realize, doesn't think of his father as a terrifying officer in Stalin's secret police. To Igor he's just an ordinary parent who works and looks after his family and makes sure they have a nice house and food.

And maybe Igor's father is not as bad as some of the others. Even in the NKVD there are probably better and worse people.

5

Flying Low

Great news!

Mr. Wilmer is driving to Tomsk in April, and he says he can take me. We'll have to stop at four or five inns along the way, but to my amazement, my mother's friend Sima sent me 500 rubles for the trip. No letter, just the money, which I had to pick up at the post office.

Now I have the travel pass, money for travel and a way of getting to Tomsk. I can hardly believe how smoothly my mission is going so far. Of course if the authorities find out I've been lying about my name and my father, it will be all over for me.

"My last name is Sokolov now," I told Mr. Wilmer when we finalized our plans.

"Understood." He didn't want to know anything more. We've all learned that the less you say about yourself or anyone else, the better.

It's easier for a kid to get away with things here. Adults get noticed, but kids can slip between the cracks.

According to Igor, every country in the war is trying to develop electronic warning systems that let soldiers know if a warplane is headed their way. In order to avoid being detected by the system, a plane has to fly very low.

That's what I have to do. Fly low. I need to be very boring, very small, nearly invisible.

I'm perfecting my "blank, innocent look." If you avoid a person's eyes, they might get suspicious. But if you look at them, they could get interested in you. So the best thing to do is act as if you're a nobody from nobody-land, as Max would say.

Speaking of Max, why hasn't he written yet? Was my letter intercepted? Did I get Max into trouble?

No, he's in Switzerland, a country that isn't even in the war. He wouldn't get into trouble no matter what I wrote. Maybe my letter got lost.

And I can't write him another letter, not now. Not until I can stop being a nobody. Letters are written by somebody.

Apart from being able to slip through the cracks because I'm a kid, it's easier to blend in and vanish in a big city like Tomsk. Half a million people live there.

Tomsk is 250 kilometers southeast of here. Mr. Wilmer said we might be able to make it in five days, if all goes well. "It's the stopping for wood that slows me down."

Mr. Wilmer's truck runs on wood instead of

gasoline. There's a big barrel right behind the cabin of his truck on the passenger side. It looks like a barrel, but it's actually a furnace and it powers the engine.

That means you can only drive for around forty-five minutes before you have to leave the main road, find a farm and buy wood chips.

On top of that, you have to pray the truck doesn't break down. Igor taught me about cars and how each part—like the brakes or the gearbox or the engine—is made up of many smaller parts. That means a lot of things can go wrong.

Now I can start storing pieces of bread for the trip. Once you dry the bread on the stove, you can keep it for a very long time.

I remember Gabi's idea of hanging the bread in a sack in the attic. She's good at that sort of thing. Collecting, storing…it's her hobby.

Gabi hasn't been going to school much lately. It's been too cold.

"Mr. Wilmer has offered me a ride to Tomsk on April 7," I tell her as soon as we're alone in the house. "I'm ready to start storing bread. Will you help me?"

"How lucky!" Gabi says.

She finds a potato sack, and we go outside, climb the ladder to the loft and hang the sack from the rafters.

"Thanks, Gabi. I need enough for ten days. Just in case."

"You'll need onions, too," Gabi says, hopping

down from the last rung of the ladder. "Otherwise you'll get scurvy."

"Listen, Gabi," I say when we're back inside.

Gabi picks up the deck of cards. We've been playing a lot of card games lately. There's nothing else to do apart from shoveling snow.

"Yes?" She hands out the cards.

"If anything happens, Gabi, you must write to me and let me know." I'm thinking about her parents. What if they get caught taking extra food or doctoring the books? I won't be around to protect her.

I had Irena when my mother was arrested, but Gabi won't have a soul if her parents are jailed. I don't want her to end up at the orphanage!

But Gabi only smiles. "Oh, you're such a worrier, Natt. Nothing's going to happen. And one day soon, the war will end."

Yes, I'm thinking. *The war will end but Stalin will still be in charge.*

Because we have two enemies. Our first enemy, Hitler, will be defeated. Ever since Hitler declared war on the United States last year, things have been going badly for the German army. They don't have a chance now of taking over Europe and then the world.

But we also have another enemy. Stalin is the one who sent my father to the Gulag, and he's the one who said we have to stay in Siberia for twenty years.

Stalin is the reason we're trying to escape.

"I win," Gabi says, throwing down her last card.

Sometimes I let Gabi win on purpose. It's a good feeling to see her smile, even if it's about something small. On top of that, I feel guilty about deserting her. She's being brave about it, but I've heard her sniffling under her blankets when she thought everyone was asleep.

I'll miss her. Gabi with her secret cave and collection of treasures and cute squinty eyes.

Maybe that's the worst part of being forced to move from place to place. You find people and then you lose them. Again and again.

6

A Change of Plan

It's my last morning in Bakchar. I'm leaving, probably forever.

Yesterday I said goodbye to Igor and Dedushka.

Igor slapped me on the back, wished me bon voyage and gave me a tiny airplane he'd carved out of wood. I made him promise not to forget about Gabi.

Dedushka looked shocked when I told him I was leaving. Then he nodded and gave me a bear hug, nearly suffocating me. He had tears in his eyes and he made me promise to write.

"Wait a minute, *umnitsa*," he said. That's what he calls me sometimes — *umnitsa*. Meaning good, clever boy. He disappeared into the cellar and came out with a small jar of strawberry jam and a bigger jar of sauerkraut.

"Be good to life, and life will be good to you," he said.

I didn't tell Mr. and Mrs. Mindru that I'm leaving. It's best if they don't know anything. But this morning I wrote them a note thanking them for their kindness. I forgive Mr. Mindru. He has a hard life, and even when he hated me, he didn't throw me out.

Now it's time to say goodbye to Gabi.

I give her the jacks and ball, the cards and rule book, the sliding puzzle, my stardust marble and my musketeer moustache.

"Here are the onions," she says, rummaging under her blankets and producing a jar of pickled chives. "I've been saving them for you. Have a good trip and thanks for the presents. And for helping me with my Russian…and for explaining the difference between dinosaurs and dragons," she adds, giggling.

"I wish you were coming with me," I say, and I mean it.

Gabi flings her arms around my shoulders and gives me a big sloppy kiss that lands on my ear. "You'd better go. You don't want to keep Mr. Wilmer waiting."

I try not to think about when and if I'll ever see Gabi again.

I walk to the outskirts of the town, the travel pass in my shirt picket, Felicia's emerald earrings in the seam of my coat, Max's life-saving hat on my head, and the sack of bread and jars of food on my back.

I also have the 500 rubles Sima sent me, which I've divided up and tucked away in my boots, under my hat, inside my coat, in my shirt pocket, and in my trouser pockets. I'll need the money for inns and for extra food if it's available. Mr. Wilmer has also asked me to contribute 50 rubles at the end of the trip to help pay for the wood chips for the truck's furnace. He's the only one who knows about the money.

I don't want to draw attention to myself, so I've left behind my down quilt. It's so tattered and moldy at this point that it's not much use anyhow. All I have, apart from the clothes on my back and the potato sack, is Max's school bag. It's nearly empty, but I can't bear to part with it.

I turned fourteen a week ago on April Fool's Day. I didn't tell anyone it was my birthday, but I did get a note from my mother. It's the only mail I've had from Mama since her first letter nearly nine months ago. I wrote to her regularly, though, with stamps generously donated by Mrs. Mindru.

Mama drew a rabbit on the note and promised that my birthday gift would be waiting for me when I saw her. I was happy that she was finally allowed to send me a letter.

I tell myself that the wind is in on my secret and is trying to pitch in by pushing me forward.

I almost laugh when I see Mr. Wilmer's truck. I hoist myself up to the passenger seat, and we're off! The next part of my mission — getting to Tomsk — will soon be completed.

The winds are getting stronger by the minute, and suddenly massive black clouds fill the sky.

Soon the wind is shaking the truck.

We can't go very fast because the road isn't paved. The ground is hard from all the hoofs and wheels that tread on it, but it's uneven, bumpy and slippery. Still, we manage to cover nearly fifty kilometers, with two very windy stops for a wood refill, before it starts to snow. Heavily.

"Our main goal now is to reach the next village," Mr. Wilmer says. He's used to driving in harsh weather, and I feel safe in his hands, but people die all the time in Siberia, five minutes from their house, because they've been blinded by a snowstorm. If the snow becomes an out-and-out blizzard and we're stuck on the road, how will we stay warm?

Luckily, we reach the village just as the snow picks up speed. I can't see anything now beyond the wild, swirling flakes.

"There's an inn down this way," Mr. Wilmer says, veering to the right. How he can make out the turn, I'm not sure, but somehow he finds it.

I jump out of the truck and Mr. Wilmer takes my arm. Without Mr. Wilmer, I'd definitely be one of those people whose lifeless body is found a few steps from a doorway.

When Mr. Wilmer said "inn," I thought back to the resorts my parents and I used to stay at when we traveled to the Carpathian Mountains. There were amazing cuckoo clocks, Persian rugs, silver dessert trays with pastries you couldn't dream up in your wildest dreams.

I didn't expect anything like that, of course, but I did expect bedrooms. Instead there's only one large room with ten plank beds. Eight of the beds have grimy straw mattresses. The remaining two don't even have that. There's no linen in sight. Just a folded army blanket on each bed.

At least no one else is here. It's only the two of us.

"This is a government facility," Mr. Wilmer explains. "Technically, Natt, you're not really allowed to be here. The inn is only for army and government personnel." He produces a voucher from his bag. "Good for one hot meal and one night," he says.

The innkeeper enters the room from an inner door.

She takes the voucher from Mr. Wilmer and says, "Don't worry, little boy."

I may be on the short side, but I'm not a little boy. Maybe her vision isn't that great. She hasn't got any teeth, and her face is as wrinkled as a withered apple.

"You can stay here," she says. "I can see you're related to Mr. Wilmer. His nephew, I assume."

Now I'm Natt Sokolov, Mr. Wilmer's nephew. On his sister's side.

"I have plenty of food," I assure Mr. Wilmer, when the old woman brings him his hot meal.

I could pay for a hot meal out of Sima's rubles,

but I don't want to waste my money, and I'm happy with my supper of dried bread, chives, sauerkraut and a teaspoon of Dedushka's strawberry jam, which is so delicious it almost hurts.

Right after the meal I poach four blankets from the empty beds and bury myself under them. A straw mattress feels luxurious after a year of sleeping on loose straw.

When I wake up in the morning, I don't want to crawl out from my warm burrow, so I stay where I am and pretend to still be asleep.

Low voices reach me from the far end of the room. I can only make out snippets of conversation: *farmer, sleigh, week at least, rubles, Tomsk, the boy.*

The boy is me.

I open my eyes and see a blonde woman in a pretty blue dress standing in the middle of the room with her hands on her waist. She catches me staring and begins to laugh. She has a very loud laugh, and when she speaks it's with a very loud voice.

"Ah, Mr. Wilmer, your nephew is awake!" she announces.

Mr. Wilmer hands me a steaming cup of white tea with a hint of sugar.

"I'm afraid I have some bad news," he says, sitting down at the edge of my bed. "It's going to be at least a week before I can continue. The storm has to pass, and then the road has to harden again. And I can't risk keeping you here for an entire week. I'll get into trouble."

I panic but try not to show it.

Mr. Wilmer sees that I'm scared.

"Don't worry, Natt," he says. "Sveta knows a farmer who can take you by sleigh. For 500 rubles he'll provide transportation, food and shelter all the way to Tomsk. He's only going as far as Melnikovo, but he'll find someone who can take you across the bridge to Tomsk."

I've never been in a passenger sleigh. In winter our mail is delivered by horse and sleigh. The postman looks snug in the cozy box cubicle under a thick blanket.

I guess it could be an adventure, traveling 200 kilometers in a sleigh. Like the North Pole expeditions Max and I used to go on, in his front yard.

7

Bedbug Hallucination

For breakfast I have my dried bread with another spoonful of strawberry jam. The jam does me more good than Dedushka could have imagined.

Sveta hands me a piece of hard cheese the size of a cranberry.

"It's important to have a good breakfast," she says in her loud, friendly voice. She looks as if she'd like to swirl around in her blue dress.

A half-hour later, a farmer arrives. He introduces himself as Stepan Stepanovitch.

But Stepan Stepanovitch doesn't have a passenger sleigh with a cozy box cubicle like the postman. He doesn't even have an open sleigh with seats.

His sleigh is nothing but a rack on blades. Everyone in Siberia uses this kind of sleigh. You put logs or heavy bags on the rack and a tired-looking horse pulls the load. If no horses are available, an adult takes their place.

And sure enough, the rack is already covered with bags of grain.

I feel as if I've been punched in the stomach. There must be some mistake.

I imagine my mother whispering over my shoulder, *Don't go, don't go.*

But Mr. Wilmer has already given the farmer my 500 rubles. I'm too embarrassed to protest now.

And maybe there really is no other choice.

Maybe I'm just being a scaredy-cat again. Igor wouldn't be afraid. I decide to be brave.

But as it turns out, I was right to worry. The sleigh ride is even worse than my worst fears.

For one thing, half the time I have to walk, because if I sit on the bags of grain for too long, I begin to freeze. The horse isn't going any faster than a human on foot.

Then, when I'm too tired to take another step, I go back to sitting on the bags.

Those are my two choices.

Freeze on the sleigh or walk myself to exhaustion in the snow.

I keep going back and forth between one and the other.

We cover fifteen kilometers, and it takes six hours, with three stops along the way to warm up, feed the poor horse and feed ourselves. At each stop Stepan

Stepanovitch buys a tiny glass of vodka, which he downs in one go.

Toward evening we arrive at a cabin on the outskirts of a small town. A thousand people seem to live in this cabin, and I'm about as welcome as a plague of locusts. Babies cry, women shout, children fight.

I'm given an old blanket and a baby to look after.

Tears stream down my face as I eat my bread.

I can't help it. I don't see how I can take two more weeks of this. At fifteen kilometers a day, that's how long it will take to get to Tomsk. And I've barely made it through today.

Mr. Wilmer said the money he gave Stepan Stepanovitch would cover food, but no one has offered me anything to eat.

It doesn't matter. I don't have much of an appetite. I'm beginning to feel feverish again, like when I first moved in with the Mindrus. But this time there's nowhere for me to recover. I have to keep going.

I cry myself to sleep on the blanket that's my bed for the night. There aren't any extra pillows, so I shove my boot under my head.

At least it's warm, and at least I'm lying down, even if it's on the floor. At least there are no mice in Siberia, or none that I've seen.

There may not be mice, but there are bedbugs. The blanket must have been crawling with them. I wake up covered with bites. It's as if I'm back on the train that brought us here. I'm so itchy I want to peel my skin off.

On the fourth day we arrive at Stepan Stepanovitch's home in Melnikovo. That's as far as he's going.

By now I feel as if I'm made of rags, like the scarecrow in *The Wizard of Oz*.

I'm more feverish than ever, and also itchier than ever, and I think I'm starting to be delirious, because when I lie down next to Stepan Stepanovitch's three small children, it seems to me that I can hear the bedbugs chattering to one another in bedbug language about the juicy boy they're going to feast on.

Stepan Stepanovitch's wife and children are the first friendly people I've met since I began the sleigh ride. His wife, Karine, is a strong-looking woman with a scar on her cheek. She sees that I'm ill, and she gives me hot cabbage and potato soup. I can barely hold the bowl. She's taken one of her children into her own bed so that I can squeeze in with the two others.

No one is going to Tomsk at the moment.

It's just as well. I spend two days in bed scratching myself half to death.

At the beginning of the third day, all of a sudden, it gets warmer. The warmer weather means that I'll be able to stay in the next sleigh the entire time. And that's a good thing, because I would not have been able to walk. I'm very weak, and my whole body feels as if it's on fire. Itchy fire.

"My uncle will take you to Tomsk," Stepan Stepanovitch tells me. I can tell he's relieved to be getting rid of me. "He'll be here soon."

The uncle leaves on what is now the eighth day since I left the Mindrus.

I stay in the sleigh for the next four days. My bag of bread vanished at Stepan Stepanovitch's, and our hosts along the way are forced to feed me. I no longer notice whether people are nice or mean.

I feel I might be dying. I'm in pain from head to foot, and at night my dreams are hot and frantic.

In one dream Papa is in our jail back home in Zastavna. Over and over I walk by him and turn my head away, like I did in real life. But in my dream, each time I turn my head, Papa grows smaller, like Alice after drinking the magic potion, until finally he's so small he's the size of my toy horse, Clop-Clop, and he can climb out through the bars, so maybe I did a good thing. Mama puts out her hands to catch him but she misses, and he falls to the ground and smashes into a hundred pieces because now he's made of wood. I watch helplessly, sick and paralyzed with horror.

I wake up and for a few seconds I'm relieved, until I remember that in real life Papa is in the Gulag and I'm traveling across Siberia on a pile of sacks while my skin feels as if needles and hot coals are pressing against it.

I'm probably not going to make it to Tomsk. I'm going to die on the way, and I'll have to be buried in the snow. Poor Mama, poor Papa. They'll be so sad that I'm gone. They'll blame themselves. But it wasn't their fault.

It was my fault. I didn't stand up for myself. I didn't say no when I saw the sleigh. I'm not a child anymore. I'm completely on my own, and if I don't look after myself, no one else will.

But it's too late now. I'm not going to last much longer.

Maybe the emerald earrings in my coat can save me — but how? No one has medicine or a truck or a decent bed. No one cares enough to look after me. They'll just take the earrings, give me soup and send me on my way before I contaminate their children.

By a miracle, when we arrive in Tomsk at noon on the twelfth day, I'm still alive — barely. Stepan Stepanovitch's uncle sees my state, and though he's barely spoken to me since we set out four days ago, something about me scares him. He can see that I'm at death's door.

I don't have a kopek on me, but he arranges for a horse and carriage to take me to Sima Israelovna's house.

While I'm in the carriage, which actually has a seat to sit on, I unbutton my coat and lift my sweater and shirt to relieve the pain of the fabric on my skin.

What I see terrifies me. My stomach is covered with red bumps or lumps, some of them small, others huge. All of them hurt.

I quickly pull my shirt back down. How can I arrive at Sima's with a dreadful disease that's probably contagious?

The cab stops in front of a three-story house. It's covered from top to bottom with white decorations that look like lace or paper snowflakes, as if it were a dollhouse.

Maybe it's another hallucination.

I walk into the dollhouse apartment building, climb a few stairs and knock on Sima's door.

And that's the last thing I remember.

8

Gibberish

At least I made it to Sima's door before I passed out. Imagine if I'd passed out on the street! No one would have known who I was or where I was going. They'd have sent me straight to an orphanage.

Instead I woke up in a hospital, and that's where I am now. Not the hospital Sima and my mother work in, which is attached to the prison, but a big hospital in Tomsk.

I'm in the infectious diseases ward with three kids and a lot of adults, most of them men. I have a skin infection on my entire body: back, neck, stomach, arms, legs.

A doctor with spectacles that keep slipping off his nose explains that I have something called Staphylococcus aureus. I got it from scratching my bites and not washing or changing my clothes for nearly two weeks.

According to him I could have easily died.

"You're very lucky the infection didn't reach your

blood and other organs," he lectures me, as if it's all my doing.

"Thank you," I say apologetically.

He nods stiffly.

"Dr. Israelovna left this for you," he says, digging into the pocket of his doctor's coat. He hands me a zippered pouch and continues on his rounds.

The pouch is made of heavy black fabric and has a hammer and sickle embroidered on it. It contains two rubles, a comb, a new toothbrush, six pills inside a pill box, and a note that says: *Iron, take one daily with meals.*

I half-remember my clothes being taken away for disinfecting, my entire body washed with some kind of chemical soap, and then my skin slathered with a cream that smells like rotten eggs. I was given a hospital shirt and robe and shown to a bed.

A real bed. Without bedbugs, covered with clean sheets instead of ragged, filthy blankets, and actually designed for the human species as opposed to, let's say, a dog or a cat, or maybe a rock.

The ward is very long and our beds are in two rows. The beds are only inches apart and there's no privacy whatsoever. You just learn very fast to turn your eyes away before you see something you will wish for the rest of your life you'd never seen.

Luckily, they've put the beds of the kids next to each other.

There are four of us: me, a boy recovering from

mumps, and two sisters, Tata and Lottie, whose lungs are "under observation."

The boy is as handsome as a movie actor and so tall and broad that he looks like a man, but he's only two months older than me. His name is Arkadi and he loves to tell jokes.

Telling jokes is extremely dangerous. Stalin has no sense of humor, and people are constantly being sent to the Gulag for making fun of life in Russia, even if they told the joke years ago.

But Arkadi's jokes are about the czars who ruled Russia before the Revolution.

I soon realize that they're really about Stalin, but Arkadi pretends that he loves Stalin.

Why did the czar pull the drowning peasant out of the lake?

So he could make sure he was loyal before throwing him back in.

He tells other kinds of jokes, too.

A man in the United States enters a capitalist's antique store. The capitalist says, "Sir, I have something very special that might interest you. It's Beethoven's skull." The man says, "That skull is too small to be Beethoven's skull." The capitalist replies, "This is Beethoven's skull when he was a child."

Thanks mostly to Arkadi, who has turned our stay here into a party, the four of us have become good friends. We have strict instructions to stay in our beds, but that doesn't stop us from having fun. We pretend we're Hollywood movie stars at a spa, and we speak Gibberish, a language we invented. Gibberish is a combination of English and nonsense. It's a silly game, but we love it, and we laugh hysterically at our Gibberish conversations.

Our only problem is food. We never get enough. We've all decided that if we don't get something more to eat we will lose our minds.

We pool our resources and find that we can scrape together just enough for a loaf of bread. But one of us will have to sneak out and buy the loaf at the market near the hospital.

And that person, everyone agrees, has to be me. I'm the shortest, the least conspicuous and, according to my three friends, "the smartest and most honest looking." I know they're flattering me so I'll agree to go, but it still feels nice to hear them say those things.

"You can have an extra slice of bread as your reward," they promise.

The problem is that I have no clothes, not even shoes. Arkadi has a nice pair of boots but they're exactly twice my size.

"Arkadi to the rescue," he says. He disappears down the corridor and returns with two sheets of newspaper, which he stuffs into the boots so they don't slide right off when I lift my feet. Everyone donates their robe and, wrapped in these four layers, I walk out of the ward and head for the exit. I prepare an excuse in case I'm stopped ("looking for a book to read") but no one pays any attention to me. The doctors and nurses are all overworked. They don't have the energy to worry about a boy strolling down the hall.

I look like I've escaped from Dr. Seward's asylum in *Dracula* as I shuffle down the street in boots twice my size and four layers of white hospital robes. But it's wonderful to be outdoors.

The sky is blue, and though it's still cold out, it's a beautiful sunny day. When I see the hospital from the outside, I can hardly believe I'm staying in such a magnificent building.

How could all those shabby little cabins of Siberia, where even a chair made of planks is a luxury, exist only a few days' ride from the majestic buildings of Tomsk?

It's like waking up from a dream, or maybe falling into one.

I follow the directions Arkadi gave me, and I soon spot the large outdoor market packed solid with booths. Customers are shouting as they try to bring down the prices. Right next to me, a man is trying to trade a music box for food. When you open the box, a tiny toy ballerina spins slowly to the sound of a harp.

The ballerina makes me think of Olga. I wonder if she still takes ballet lessons.

I buy the bread as quickly as I can at the first booth that has baked goods. I pretend no one is actually looking at me, and my practice of being invisible serves a whole new purpose, saving me from total humiliation.

I hurry back to the ward, and we all pounce on the bread. I get my extra slice as promised.

I've lost a lot of weight since leaving Bakchar. I didn't know I had any weight to lose, but it seems I did. Now if the doctors want to teach their students about human ribs, they can count mine.

"I used to be pretty chubby," I tell Arkadi. "Believe it or not."

"I used to know what food looked like," Arkadi replies with a snicker.

Then he asks about my skin disease. He knows it isn't contagious as long as he doesn't touch me, but he's curious about how I got it.

I tell him the whole story of my trip to Tomsk. How I started off in Mr. Wilmer's truck, but then because of the snow I had to switch to the sleigh.

When I've finished, Arkadi folds his arms and declares, "That makes absolutely no sense, Natan." That's my name in Russian. Same as Hebrew, but with the emphasis on the first syllable: NA-tan.

"What doesn't make sense?"

"The entire story. Look, if you'd stayed for a week in that village where you were snowed in and then continued in the truck, the whole trip would have taken you twelve days and only cost you a maximum of twenty-five rubles for accommodation. It only costs two or three rubles to sleep on someone's floor."

Can that be true? Does basic shelter cost so little?

"Going by sleigh," he continues, "took you just as long and cost you 500 rubles. For what? You say you barely ate, so where did it all go? You were duped, my friend. And almost died in the process."

Tata and Lottie nod their heads. "*Plutuberson, yes*," they say in Gibberish/English.

"I'm not sure there was anywhere for me to stay in that tiny village," I say.

"There's always a way to squeeze in one more person," Arkadi insists. "We Russians are geniuses at packing ourselves like sardines into whatever rooms are available."

And he begins to list possible explanations for the change of plan from truck to sleigh. In most of his guesses, Mr. Wilmer is either a liar, a thief or both.

I know he's wrong. Mr. Wilmer would never trick me.

He told me he gave Stepan Stepanovitch the 500 rubles to cover transportaion, the beds (or blankets) for the night and extra food.

Food is the most precious thing there is in Russia, now that there's a war on, and that makes it expensive. People give away everything they have — clothes, shoes, watches, gramophones, lace, sewing machines — in exchange for cabbages and kasha and beets.

Mr. Wilmer didn't know I'd lose my appetite, or that some of the hosts wouldn't offer me anything to eat.

But I don't mind listening to Arkadi's wild theories. He's always funny, no matter what he's ranting about.

"Did you say there was a woman there when he told you about the arrangement with Stepan Stepanovitch? Maybe she wanted a ride to Tomsk so he had to get rid of you. Maybe she's his girlfriend. Or maybe someone offered him a big chunk of money for a lift to Tomsk. He couldn't ask you for more than the 50 rubles you'd already agreed to. Maybe he pocketed some of your money himself and only gave Stepan Stepanovitch a fraction of what you had. Any way you look at it, my friend, the wool was pulled over your eyes."

"He didn't know the sleigh ride would be so bad," I say. "He always brought me treats when he returned from his trips…"

"Oh, he didn't know that sitting on bags of grain for 200 kilometers in April would be a disaster? As opposed to waiting a week indoors and then continuing by truck? Yes, maybe he was only born two days ago…"

I have to admit that Arkadi has a point. Mr. Wilmer must have known that it would take just as long to travel by sleigh as it would have if I'd waited for the roads to improve and then continued in the truck with him.

He must have known that going to Tomsk by truck would cost less, and that I'd be comfortable and warm.

If only Irena were here! She'd know exactly what was what.

I miss her. She never wrote, so I can't even send her my new address.

Elias and Cecilia would have known, too. Even Mrs. Mindru would have been able to tell me what was going on. But they've all vanished from my life.

After a week in the ward, thanks to the evil-smelling cream, I'm cured.

Sima comes to pick me up. She turns out to be a slightly scary woman with black-framed glasses. Scary because she's so stern and serious. She's wearing a pretty braided green sweater which I recognize immediately as one of my mother's creations.

I say goodbye to Arkadi and Tata and Lottie. *"Thank you spoolfilly you're welcome it has been utriskabish to know you fliggitin goodbye.*"

"*Uggrushpibble, uggrushpibble,*" Arkadi says, shaking my hand. Tata and Lottie join in. "*Uggrushpibble! Goodbye, Hollywood!*"

9

Aunt Sima and Grandmother Natasha

"You can call me Aunt Sima," Sima says as we walk out to the street. "You're looking much better! Ah, yes, you're noticing the sweater. Your mother made it for me, as you've guessed. Are you up to a bit of a walk? I have to pick up a few things at the market and you can help me carry them home. I live with my mother. You can call her Grandmother Natasha. From now on, you're my nephew."

How many uncles and aunts from different families can one boy have!

But I nod. "Thank you for everything. For bringing me to the hospital and the —"

But Sima interrupts me. "Let's focus on the present," she says.

I feel ashamed. For a few seconds I forgot that everything we're doing could land us in huge and terrible trouble. And here on the street, anyone could overhear our conversation.

We walk to the market. I hope no one remembers the boy in the enormous boots and four hospital robes. At least this time I'm wearing my ordinary clothes, and even though they're stained and patched up, they've been cleaned and they actually fit me.

Sima shops, and I hold the two knitted shopping bags for her.

The walk back to her place feels very long. My legs are weak, and I'm carrying a heavy bag of flour. Sima's bags look even heavier.

Finally we reach her house, with its snowflake decorations.

Sima explains that the house is divided into six apartments, each with two small rooms and a bathroom. Sima's apartment, luckily, is on the first floor. I wouldn't have been able to climb more than a few stairs.

"We have many neighbors," she says. "We're all members of the Communist Party."

I nod. Many neighbors, and you can't trust anyone.

Sima knocks on the door five times in what is clearly a code—two raps, then one, then another two. We hear movement inside, then the lock is turned and a pair of eyes peer through the chained gap. The owner of the eyes shuts the door again and slides the chain back to let us in.

I enter the small apartment and almost gasp. I've

quite simply forgotten what a home with white clapboard walls and a sofa looks like.

The wall above the sofa is covered with the usual portraits of the fathers of Communism: Marx, Engels and especially Lenin.

At this point I've seen so many pictures of Lenin at different stages of his life that I feel I know him personally. Lenin as a baby, Lenin boarding a train to exile, Lenin returning from exile, Lenin in prison, Lenin writing his revolutionary works, Lenin with a lantern, Lenin surrounded by children, playing with children, helping children. The photo on Sima's wall shows Lenin teaching a little girl how to write. It's one of my favorites, because the girl reminds me of Lucy, the sweet-smelling dentist's daughter from back home. I'm happy to see it here.

There's also a portrait of Stalin, of course. It's bigger than the others, but as soon as the door is shut and locked, Natasha lifts a tall spiky plant from the floor and places it on a little side table, where it mostly hides Stalin's face.

Risky!

But people have to knock and wait before they enter, giving Sima and Natasha plenty of time to move the plant back to the floor.

Natasha looks more like Sima's sister than her mother. She's also wearing something Mama made for her—a red-and-white dress. It makes me feel good to see it, on top of everything else in this enchanted place.

"It's like a castle here," I say.

They both laugh. Here at home, Sima isn't quite as scary. I still wouldn't want to get on her wrong side, though.

"So you're Sophie's little boy," Natasha says, shaking my hand.

Little, again! But I don't mind. I don't mind anything right now. I'm in paradise.

"You can call me Gran," she says. "Where are you in your schooling?"

"Oh, give him time to settle in, Mother," Sima says.

"I like your name," I say. "I read *War and Peace*."

Natasha looks impressed. "All of it?"

I nod. "I didn't have anything else to read. Just an English primer. I know it by heart. *Fine weather today*," I add in English.

They both laugh again. Natasha has a few gold teeth.

Sima hands me a bar of soap. I stare at it in a bit of a daze. I haven't seen a bar of soap in I don't know how long. I think I remember how to use it...

"Only one book?" Natasha continues. "Well, we shall have to do something about that. Tomorrow I'll take you to the library, and we'll discuss your schooling, too."

Sima shows me to the shower. The apartment is small, but the modern plumbing, right there in the apartment, makes me feel like a prince.

I take a very quick shower with tepid water. I still have small scars on my body, but the infection is completely gone.

10

Mama

Soon, very soon, my mother is going to be released from prison. I don't want to get too excited, because I've heard about people who are told on the day of their release that they have to stay in jail for another year. Or two. Or ten.

But Sima says my mother is in everybody's good books, and that there's "every chance" she really will be released.

By now I'm used to living without my mother, but I know how hard it's been for her to live without me. And how hard her life must be. Poor Mama!

So I was happy when Sima returned from work yesterday and announced, "Natt, I've arranged for you to visit your mama tomorrow at noon."

It's a half-hour walk to the prison. My directions are to "follow the railway line, you can't miss it — but don't get too close to the tracks!"

While I walk, I think about what I'll say. I decide to be calm and controlled during the visit. Otherwise

Mama will think I've spent the last year crying my-self to sleep because I missed her so much.

The truth is that there were days and even weeks when I barely thought about my mother. I feel a bit guilty about it, but she began to fade from my life. It happened partly because it made me too sad to think about her and partly because I'm not a little kid anymore.

Mostly I want to reassure her that I'm doing well. And I really am doing well. My life right now is the best it's been since we left home. I'm in a big city and staying in Sima's apartment, where there's food, a shower and a modern flush toilet. Instead of doing miserable chores from morning to night, I spend my days reading books in a beautiful library.

It's sunny and warm out, and the snow on the ground is starting to shrink. I can hear the birds sing-ing in the forest and I whistle along with them.

I arrive at the prison at noon on the dot and go straight to the main office. When I tell the guard who I am, I almost make a dreadful mistake. I almost say, *I'm Natt Sokolov*. But at the very last second, I remember that here I'm still Natt Silver. Close call!

"My name is Natt So—Silver. I'm here to see my mother, Sophie Silver," I say as politely as possible.

"Wait outside!" the guard barks without looking up.

Is this how the guards talk to Mama? I can't bear to think of Mama being shouted at and bullied. My good mood evaporates, and a sinking feeling of help-lessness and worry takes its place.

A long time passes, and I'm sure they've forgotten all about me, and that when they remember, they're going to send me home.

But finally, after nearly an hour, a woman in uni-form comes out of the office and says, "Natt Silver? Go to the guard house, comrade. You'll see your mother there." To my immense relief, she doesn't speak to me the way the guard at the main office did.

In fact, even though she's trying to sound formal, I sense that she knows my mother and is happy for her.

I make my way to a cabin near the gate. There's a bench inside, and I'm grateful to be sitting at last.

After a few minutes, my mother appears.

She looks so different that for a split second I'm not sure it's her. Her hair is cut very short and there are deep lines on her forehead and between her eyebrows. Her mouth is thinner, and her face seems to have fallen somehow. Even her hands, which are gripping a package, have changed. They're rough and swollen and there's a bandage on one of her fingers.

Mama smiles with relief when she sees me, and tears roll down her cheeks.

She sits next to me and I hug her for a long time. She almost chokes on her sobs.

She's no longer the one who comforts and looks

after me. She's the one who needs looking after. It's as if I'm the parent now.

Finally she calms down. "You look so much older, my darling," she says in Russian. We've never spoken Russian to one another, only German. But we have no choice now.

"Everything is going well," I tell her. "Very well."

"I have a birthday present for you, dearest," she says, handing me the package. It's heavier than I expected. "Do you have enough to eat?"

"I've been eating very well." There's so much more to say, but the guard is listening to every word.

"Darling, you must find a room for us to live in when I come out. We have to register as residents of Tomsk."

I nod. More instructions.

Our fifteen minutes are up, and I'm ordered to leave the room while Mama is checked for weapons. How could I have slipped her a weapon when the guard's hawk eyes were on us every second? And what exactly would she do with a weapon?

But the rules aren't there to make sense. They're there to remind us who's in charge.

As I walk back to Sima's, I try to sort out the jumble of confused feelings swirling around in my brain.

Mostly I'm sad for Mama. Yes, she has an indoor job, and Sima has been kind to her, and even the guard who showed me to the cabin seems to like her.

But she looks so pitiful, and I can tell she's had a miserable time in prison.

I'm also sad, in a way, that she's no longer the person who looks after me and protects me from bad things. She wants to be that person, but Siberia has made her as fragile as a ladybug on a leaf. At the same time, this means that I'm the strong one now, and it's good to be strong.

And I'm glad because I know the visit meant the world to Mama. It must have been torture for her to be separated from me. I hope she received my letters, at least. I wish now that I'd written more often.

But the best part is that soon she'll be released. Don't worry, Mama. I'll look after you till the day I die!

I remember that I'm holding my birthday present. I undo the brown paper wrapping and peek inside.

It's a kilo of sugar! Enough for at least a month of cookies and cakes. Mama must have knitted a hundred sweaters for a kilo of sugar.

I pick up my pace.

11

Living on a Shelf

On the day of her release, Mama comes home with Sima.

The first thing she does is take a shower.

"I'm in heaven," she calls out from behind the shower curtain, and we all laugh.

Then she has tea and cookies (made with her sugar), and we hug and share stories and talk about our plans.

I've been asking everyone I meet if they know of a room for rent, and Sima's been asking everyone she knows, but so far we haven't had any luck.

Mama and I spend the next few days roaming the city in search of a room. But no one wants to rent to us.

Finally, at the beginning of July, a shopkeeper tells us about the Professor.

"My aunt is moving out of her room tomorrow," the shopkeeper says, scribbling down an address. "Ask for the Professor."

The Professor is a gaunt, heavily bearded man who may have been a professor once but is now tattered and dusty. He's the superintendent of a complex of three-story buildings that face a central courtyard.

"What do you want?" he says when we approach him. He's sitting on the ground with his back against a wall and his eyes closed. There's an empty bottle of vodka by his side.

"We heard someone is moving out. Is her room available?" my mother asks politely.

"Left this morning," he says, slurring his words. Then he picks up the empty bottle, tries to drink from it and swears when he realizes it's empty.

"Take it if you want," he shrugs and goes back to sleep.

Success at last!

The room is three meters wide and four meters long. It's up one flight of stairs and right next to a storeroom filled with logs. It has a small woodstove and an iron bed.

The best thing about it is a large shelf hanging from the ceiling. The shelf is half the size of the room.

I can sleep on the shelf and Mama can sleep on the iron bed.

This is a good system until October.

Suddenly, at the end of October, the room gets very, very cold. Mama has to join me on the shelf because it's slightly less cold near the ceiling. Down below, whatever water remains in our two pails turns to ice overnight. The small stove gives off about as much heat as a candle.

Even on the shelf, where we're bundled up in our coats and blankets, we're constantly shivering. Sometimes we're so cold our teeth chatter. How will we survive the worst months?

I'd love to move in with Sima and Natasha. Their place is always warm. But I can't desert Mama. And she has to have a place of her own so she can register as a Tomsk resident. Once she's a resident, she can apply for permission to leave. That's the next step in our escape plan.

My mother needs me. She needs someone to fill our two pails with water every morning, and to chop wood from the storeroom for our stove. She needs someone to keep her company. She'd miss me too much if I lived anywhere else.

On top of that, she doesn't think we should impose on Sima any longer. Sima's taken enough risks for us.

But my new friend, Yuri, tells me he can solve our temperature problem.

Yuri is the son of Mrs. Popov, an innkeeper who's been a great friend to my mother since she came out of prison. Mrs. Popov heard about my mother's knitting while my mother was still in jail, and she ordered a vest. Now she advertises my mother's knitting services, finds her excellent customers and lets my mother meet and measure the customers at her inn.

And I've become pals with Mrs. Popov's son.

Yuri is a thin athletic guy whose dream is to be a 100-meter sprinter at the Olympics. He wanted to be a swimmer, but he didn't have anywhere to swim on a regular basis. Sprinting you can practice anywhere. He's already up (or down) to 16 seconds. The Olympic world record, I now know, is Eddie Tolan in 1932, 10.3 seconds.

"What you need is an electric burner," Yuri tells me. We're in his attic room at the inn, looking at his sports scrapbooks. "You know, a hot plate. It will keep you warm, and you can heat water on it."

"But we don't have a plug in our room."

"Leave it to me."

The next morning he shows up at our little room with a hot plate and a little box of tools.

My mother is just on her way out. She's rarely home during the day. The room is too cold, and besides, Mama likes to socialize while she knits. So she takes her knitting to Sima's, or Mrs. Popov's, or even the library.

When my mother leaves, Yuri climbs up to the platform, takes a little knife from his toolbox and shows me how to scrape the insulation from the wires that run along the ceiling.

"You have to be careful. If the wires touch, you get a big fizzle-sizzle-boom short circuit," he explains as I watch nervously.

I'm wondering if we're the ones who are going to fizzle-sizzle as the entire building burns down in an electric fire. But Yuri seems very sure about what he's doing.

Once he's finished with the ceiling wires, he exposes the ends of the hotplate wires, bends them into hooks and attaches them onto the ceiling wire.

And voilà, the hotplate comes on!

"What if the super notices that our room is taking up more electricity than the other rooms?" I ask. "We're only allowed this 25-watt bulb."

"From what you've told me about your superintendent, you have nothing to worry about," Yuri says, grinning. "Besides, how do you think everyone else is not freezing to death? Now I'll show you what to do if you get a short circuit."

We go out to the corridor, and Yuri points out the fuse box. But we have to wait until no one is around.

Finally the coast is clear. Yuri assigns me the job of lookout and opens the fuse box. He laughs when he sees what's inside.

"If this is a fuse, I'm Napoleon Bonaparte," he chuckles. He shows me how to repair the "so-called fuse" with a thin piece of copper wire if it short-circuits.

Since I have no idea what a fuse is supposed to look like, I don't exactly know what he's talking about, but I learn to do what he does.

Yuri invites me to join him for lunch at the inn, but I need to be here when Mama comes back.

"Don't kiss a porcupine!" he shouts as he runs off.

When he's gone, I try to read. But I'm too worried.

On the one hand, what if we get caught? It's true that the Professor won't know or care, but what if someone else finds out?

On the other hand, it's a matter of life and death. If it's this cold in November, we won't last the winter without extra heating.

When Mama comes home, she's amazed at how warm the room is. I show her Yuri's ingenious trick.

"Oh, darling, I don't think it's allowed," she whispers anxiously.

"The Professor won't notice," I say, echoing Yuri. "He doesn't know if it's night or day."

"But what if an inspector comes…or someone sees it when we open the door? You know how nosy people can be."

"Stop being such a scaredy-cat!" I say. My anger takes me by surprise, especially because I'm nowhere near as confident as I'm pretending to be. I don't think I've ever been this rude to my mother, but I can't help it.

"I can't live this way!" I hiss. "I'm sick of being a

ghost! This is a good thing, and you're turning it into a bad thing."

"Hush, hush, darling," Mama says, trying to squeeze my hand.

I pull my hand away and stomp out of the room.

But it only takes me a few minutes to regret every word I said. Who can blame Mama for being scared, after what she's been through?

I return to the room to apologize, but my mother beats me to it.

"I'm sorry, darling. I have no right to ask you to freeze. And after all," she continues, "I'm now making clothes for some very important officers in the NKVD and their wives and children, too. I have connections…"

"Yes, it will be okay," I mumble. No need to add that everyone in Russia takes risks because if you followed every rule, you'd be dead in a week. She already knows that.

"How clever of Yuri!" she exclaims as cheerfully as she can. But she's not as good at acting as she used to be.

Our evenings are much more pleasant now. The hot plate gets red hot, and Mama and I no longer have to wear our winter coats indoors.

I know the whole setup isn't safe. The wires on the ceiling are very old, and the insulation is cracked and missing in a lot of places.

I must say I'm becoming quite the expert at fixing the fuse. I always carry a book in case anyone sees me. I can say I'm visiting my neighbor, Nadeja Michailovna.

But Yuri isn't finished with his improvements.

Our window looks out to the inner courtyard where the speakers blare out propaganda all day long. Between the speeches there's music: jazz, choirs singing popular songs, opera, orchestra pieces. Yuri brings over a small loudspeaker (I don't know where he finds these things) and draws a double wire through the window into the yard, where he attaches the wires by climbing a pole that runs the radio transmission wires.

Then he builds a switch on our private loudspeaker so we can shut off the propaganda and turn it back on when there's music.

"Now whenever you hear 'We'll Meet Again' you'll think of me," Yuri jokes.

12

Fourth Letter to Max

December 12, 1943
Hi Max,

Natt Sokolov here. I still haven't heard from you, and I don't know if my last letter reached you. I won't send you my address this time, because I'm not sure how long I'll be here. Right now I'm in the beautiful city of Tomsk. My father has been wounded while serving in the Red Army. He is now recovering. I'm waiting for him here.

I have a lot of news. First of all, I'm in grade 4! At my age, can you imagine? But I'm not the only one. There are other kids my age in the class, and two who are even older. That makes it easier.

I think I'll be able to skip to grade 9 pretty soon, thanks to an 83-year-old woman who lives next door to where I'm staying. Her name is Nadeja Michailovna, and she's a retired teacher. She's a very elegant sort of person, like someone out of a book. She's teaching me all the required subjects. She's also teaching me about music, famous paintings and all the other arts. She was born the same year as Chekhov, Gustav Mahler, Herzl and the guy who wrote Peter Pan! She owns a piano and can still play it.

There's a wonderful library here and I'm eating up the books. The librarian helps me. I'm reading lots of French literature (in Russian of course): Victor Hugo, Balzac, de Maupassant, Zola...and of course all the Russians. Even some of our old favorites, like Jack London and Mark Twain. Nadeja Michailovna also has beautiful old books, and she's taught me how to read the old Russian script. I love Gorky. He wrote about his sad childhood. We have a lot in common, me and Gorky.

My mother is making a good living knitting. Remember those dresses she knit for your sisters, and your blue sweater? Well, all that practice has come in handy. She now knits for everyone, and she even has a waiting list. Wool clothes are in high demand here because of the cold. I read out loud to her as she knits in the evening, which helps the time pass.

We live on a platform. Basically it's a shelf that hangs from the ceiling. It's a big shelf, long enough for Andreas the Tall to stretch out if he was here, and around the same width. So that's where my mother sits and knits in the evening, and I read to her, the two of us leaning against the wall, our heads inches from the ceiling. Right now we're reading Crime and Punishment, about a murder. It's really good. You'd like it.

We also sleep on the platform, cocooned in our blankets.

We even keep our potatoes on the shelf, in a box I built. We tried storing them in a neighbor's cellar, but they froze and rotted. My mother nearly cried. Potatoes are like gold here. So now we keep them with us on the shelf. To prevent all three of us from crashing down — me, my mother and the potatoes — I installed a wooden post under the shelf for support. We have a small bulb hanging from the ceiling and of course sunlight during the day.

I forgot to tell you that I met that ancient fortune teller from Zastavna before we boarded the train to Siberia! She knew me, and she remembered you.

Anyhow, she read my palm. She said my family would make it through the war and that we'd all reunite when it ended. No one can really see the future, of course, but somehow it made me feel better.

I have to get back to my math. School is very different here. Remember how Comrade Martha told us not to bow, because we were all equal? Well, here we have to bow to our teachers, and if we run into them in the street we have to bow plus take off our hat. We also have to be clean, comb our hair, sit up straight, obey without question, help the little kids, etc. Otherwise we get into trouble. But Comrade Martha was right about one thing — teachers aren't allowed to hit us. I also get a free hot meal (usually kasha) every day, because my father is in the Red Army.

I had a very long sleigh ride to Tomsk that I'll tell you

about when I see you again. I can't wait for that day to come. I want to hear about everything you've been doing.

Regards to your family.

Your friend, Natt

THREE
ESCAPE

1944
WINTER

1

Born in Bucharest

It's Saturday, January 22, but thanks to Yuri, Mama and I aren't turning into blocks of ice in our little room. We're listening to a program devoted to the Russian composer Rimsky-Korsakov. The music is so lively that we're humming along and pretending we know the melody.

Suddenly we hear a voice shouting our names through the door. I freeze for a second, but it's only Sima.

"Sophie, Natt, I have something for you!" she calls out.

We climb down from the platform, turn off our hot plate and loudspeaker and hurry out to the corridor.

Sima hands my mother a letter.

It's from Papa!

We haven't had a word from Papa in two and a half years. Mama saw him at his trial, but I haven't seen him for over three years.

My mother is shaking like a leaf and laughing in

a wild, gasping way that sounds more like a squawk than a laugh. She's shaking too much to open the envelope so she hands it to me, but I'm shaking, too, and in the end Sima has to tear open the envelope and read the letter to us, because our tears are blurring our vision.

My beloved Sophie and beloved son, I write to you with good news. An agreement has been reached to release some Romanian citizens, and since I was born and grew up in Bucharest, I will be allowed to return to my home. I plan to be in Moscow, on my way to Bucharest, within two months. I will send you money by postal order and hope to see you very soon. I am well and have been working as an accountant for the mines. I think of you every minute of every hour. I am sorry I was not able to write sooner. Your loving husband and father.

"You'd better come over and we can share the news with my mother," Sima says, her voice as careful and controlled as it always is when she's outside her home.

So the three of us head over to Sima's place, where we drink tea and read Papa's letter again and again. Every time we come to the words, *since I was born and grew up in Bucharest*, we burst out laughing.

My father has never been to Bucharest in his life. But he does know Romanian, and he's managed to persuade the people in charge that he qualifies for release.

His original sentence was twenty years, like ours.

And now I can say it out loud. Many people don't survive the Gulag prisons of Siberia. And Papa was sent to Magadan, one of the coldest cities on the planet.

But he survived, because at least for part of the time, he had an indoor job, like Mama. His talent for accounting saved his life.

"But how can he possibly have money?" Mama wonders. "And how can he get to a post office to send it? I don't understand…"

It does seem impossible. A Gulag prisoner with extra money going to a post office to send a money order to relatives, as opposed to trying not to starve to death? It's more than strange.

But Stalin's Russia is full of strange things.

"How lucky that he received your letter!" Mama beams at Sima. "Once again I am more indebted to you than I can say."

A letter from a member of the Communist Party was safer and more likely to reach my father than a letter from another prison, so Sima sent Papa a short note, giving him news about imaginary relatives and adding, *Sophie Sokolov, Natt's mother, is working for me at the moment.* He understood.

We discuss what to do next.

Mama's been going to the police station every day, trying to get a permit that says she lives in Tomsk. Without that permit, she can't apply for permission to leave the city.

The police ask her the same questions over and over. Every evening I drill her on the answers.

"Just stick to your story. Don't add anything, don't change anything," I tell her.

Her story is that she was in Bucovina when her husband was drafted into the Red Army, and her documents were stolen. Papers get stolen all the time here.

The interrogations last for hours, and Mama's nerves are in pieces. But there's no going back now.

"You're fantastic at pretending," I remind her. "Remember how you impressed that chief in Zastavna when I was arrested?"

I spent a day in jail just before we were exiled, because the NKVD thought Mama was hiding. When my mother showed up to get me, she had to persuade the chief of police that she'd only been visiting a friend. She practically made him think she was in love with him.

Mama smiles and says, "Thank God the right hand doesn't know what the left hand is doing. They have no idea who I am."

In other words, the authorities can't keep track of who was in prison and who wasn't. Luckily, no one has recognized her.

"As soon as you have the Tomsk permit, I'll get the papers we need," I announce.

Mama looks doubtful. "How? It's almost impossible to get permission to travel without a connection."

"I have a connection," I reply.

Because once again, as in Bakchar, I'm on good terms with someone in the NKVD.

2

Gennady

There's a boy in my class who has a round face, round glasses and round dimples when he smiles, which is most of the time. I've been tutoring him for a few months. He's actually very clever, and when we go over the exercises at his home, he understands and remembers everything. It's only in the classroom that he can't seem to learn much.

His name is Gennady Gordeev, and he's thirteen. He lives in a big old-style apartment that rich people used to live in before the Revolution. Before the Revolution, millions of peasants were starving so the rich could get richer. After the Revolution, the expensive furniture and chandeliers and silverware became the property of the State, and the big houses were divided up into smaller units.

But this apartment somehow escaped the Revolution. It still has chandeliers and fancy furniture.

Gennady has his own room and lots of toys and games. His mother is so pleased with his progress —

he's now getting 5, the top mark, in all his tests — that she always gives me a hot meal. Before my tutoring, Gennady rarely got more than 1 (very poor) or 2 (poor).

After homework, it's time for fun. Gennady has tanks, a Red Cross ambulance, a bulldozer, a crane, three tractors, a train set, toy soldiers and a huge collection of board games: Chemical War, Sea Battle, Modern Battle, Tank Battle, Traveling Along the Riches of the USSR, Electrification, Maneuvers of a Pioneer Group, Let's Give Raw Materials to the Factories.

We get so involved in our games that we play right up to his bedtime.

Imagine having a bedtime, instead of waiting all day for the blissful moment when you can finally lay your head on a pillow and shut your eyes.

That used to be me long ago — a kid with a bedtime.

On one of my early visits, Mrs. Gordeev admired my sweater, and when I told her about my mother's waiting list, she became very interested. My mother pushed her to the front of the line and immediately knit her a sweater. Mrs. Gordeev was thrilled with it.

The strange coincidence is that Gennady's father is a major in the NKVD. For the second time, I'm a welcome guest in the house of an officer in the secret police.

Unlike Igor's father, he's often at home, and we've had quite a few conversations. That is, Mr. Gordeev talks, mostly about his childhood, and I listen. He had to overcome a lot of adversity: being poor, a dead mother, a drunk father, a cruel brother, a sick sister, a bad-tempered horse and a moustache that wouldn't grow evenly.

So I gather my courage and the next time he asks me, "How are you, young man?" I plunge in.

"We just heard from my father, who was wounded in the Red Army," I say. "He wants us to join him."

I'm getting so used to the tall tale that for a minute I almost believe it myself.

"Brave man," Mr. Gordeev nods.

"My mother and I need permission to leave Tomsk. Can you advise us, please?"

"Hmm…maybe I can help. I will let you know, my dear boy," he says.

That sounds promising. But his reply, a few days later, is the last thing I expect.

Gennady and I are playing checkers when his father calls the two of us into the living room. He's sitting in his royal-looking armchair with a glass of reddish liquid in his huge hands.

"I've been promoted to Colonel," he announces proudly. "Gennady, we're going to be moving to Vladivostok. Would you like Natt to come with us?"

"Yes!" Gennady nods vigorously.

"Well, then, Natan, we'd like to invite you to come with us as Gennady's permanent tutor and brother. Yes, we'd like to adopt you. We promise to take the best possible care of you. You will be a son to us. I'm sure your mother will be enthusiastic when she hears about this opportunity."

In spite of myself, I'm moved, and I even feel bad for him. I have to remind myself who I'm feeling bad for—a member of the same secret police that arrested my father and his friends for no reason and sent them all to the Gulag.

I know I need to be very diplomatic.

"Oh, that would be such an honor, sir. And I wish I could come with you, it would give me the greatest pleasure. But my father is expecting me, and I can't let him down. He's been such a hero in the army, and it would be a terrible blow to him."

Gennady nods. He understands. A boy can't just get up and join another family on request.

But his father frowns. He clearly expected me to jump at the offer.

So much for Mr. Gordeev. He's not going to help us now.

Time for Plan B.

3

Plan B

Dear Olga and Peter,

I hope you are both well and having fun. Life here continues to be very busy for me with homework, exams, friends, tutoring, movies and so on. I came top in my class in chemistry, which gives you an idea of how hard I was studying.

I don't know if I ever mentioned it, but my father was serving in the Red Army and has been wounded. He's recovering in Moscow and would like me and my mother to join him there in the spring. I'm wondering if you know of anyone who could help us get the papers we need? My mother is a permanent resident of Tomsk, and we've saved enough money for the train. We'd be taking the train to Novosibirsk first, and it would be great to see you again. It's so long since we first met but I remember it as though it was yesterday. I hope you don't mind the request.

Your penpal and friend, Natt Sokolov

Hello Natt!

It was splendid as always to hear from you, old pal.

How excellent that you are planning to come to Novosibirsk in the spring! We would love to see you, old pal, and you and your mother would be welcome to stay with us for as long as you need to. We showed Father your letter and he says your Russian is "beautiful" so there's a compliment for you to have with your supper! The papers are not a problem. Just go to the enclosed address and ask for Sergei Petrov. He will be expecting you. Hope to see you soon!

Your friends,
Peter and Olga

4

Leaving Tomsk

Somehow, we did it.

We got the residence passport for Tomsk.

Then, thanks to Peter and Olga's father, we got travel permits for Sophia Sokolov and Natan Sokolov, allowing us to travel to Moscow.

Mama has saved 2,000 rubles from her knitting, and Papa sent us 1,000 rubles. We still don't know how he managed it.

We're now ready to leave Tomsk.

In the morning, Mrs. Popov and Yuri come over to Sima's apartment to say goodbye. We couldn't have made it this far without Sima and Natasha and Mrs. Popov. We might not even be alive if not for them.

It's hard saying goodbye to Yuri. Thanks to him we were warm and had music and I learned about electricity and sprinting.

That joke he made—about thinking of him when I hear the song "We'll Meet Again"—keeps coming back to me. It's a joke but it's also true. I don't know where or when I'll be seeing anyone. I'm leaving them all behind.

Yuri is sad, too. He gives me a big bear hug.

"Don't forget me, friend," he says. "You know my address!"

Back home, I drop in at Nadeja Michailovna's one last time, and she gives me one of her books, *Lives of the Great Composers*.

"The great always suffer," she says.

Just before I leave, she begins to cry.

"Don't pay attention to me," she says. "I'm very happy for you." Then she leans forward and kisses my forehead.

I haven't said goodbye to any of my classmates or teachers. We haven't even told the superintendent that we're leaving. As usual, the less others know, the better.

We get rid of the hot plate, sleep for a few hours, then wake up at 3:00 a.m. to pack our clothes, most of which have been mended so often it's impossible to guess what they once looked like. With my tutoring money I bought three packs of cigarettes to use as bribes, and I shove them into my pocket.

"I'm taking Yuri's loudspeaker," I whisper to my mother. There's plenty of room in the suitcases. We've sold almost everything we owned.

My mother is about to protest, but changes her mind, smiles sleepily and nods her head.

Our two small suitcases, which we bought from another tenant, are so old and torn we have to tie them with rope. We tie the end of the rope to our wrists, so that no one can steal them.

No matter how shabby your things are, there's always someone who will be ready to take them off your hands — literally.

Mama stuffs half our money inside her shirt, and I stuff the other half in my boots.

I also have a reference letter from Gennady's mother. A letter from his father would have been better, but I didn't dare ask him after I rejected his offer to adopt me. Mrs. Gordeev, however, wrote me a gushing reference letter, like something out of a novel, and she included her husband's name.

My husband, Colonel Alexander Gordeev, and I were overwhelmed by the improvement in our son's grades...

Followed by about twenty adjectives describing my heroic tutoring.

But the most precious item of all is a secret gift for Olga. I've hidden it inside Sima's zippered hammer-and-sickle pouch, which is hanging from a cord around my neck.

I'd heard rumors all winter that there were stores where you could get chocolate for your meat ration. I went from store to store, week after week, month after month, until finally, by miracle, I found one that had just received a shipment of American chocolate bars. Sure enough, they were ready to give me a small wrapped chocolate bar for my meat ration. The print on the wrapper is in English and it says *US Army Field Ration D*.

I can't wait to see Olga's face when I give it to her.

We arrive at the Tomsk railway station just after 5:00 a.m. It's still dark out, but the waiting room is already packed. You can't book specific trains in advance, because no one knows which trains will come when.

All you can do is buy tickets for the distance you need. Then you just have to wait. Sometimes you have to wait for days, sleeping on the floor of the waiting room before the right train arrives.

There's a tap with boiling water in the corridor, and Mama and I fill our mugs and dip the dried bread we brought with us into the hot water.

My mother spots the stationmaster and gives him her biggest smile.

"So sorry to trouble you," she says. "But do you know if there will be a train to Novosibirsk this week?"

"You're in luck, comrade. There's a train to Novosibirsk leaving today," he replies.

"Is it a passenger train?" I ask. "Or a Happy Train?"

A Happy Train is a cargo train with empty carriages, and it has that name because people who ride on it are just happy to finally be on their way, no matter how windy and uncomfortable they're going to be. The main thing is that after endless waiting, they're actually moving.

"I have no idea," the stationmaster replies and continues on his way.

But we really are in luck. In the early afternoon, a real passenger train headed for Novosibirsk pulls into the station. We grab our luggage and join the mad rush onto the platform. I'm afraid I'll be separated from Mama.

"Hold on tight, Mama. Don't let go of me, no matter what."

There are two police officers at the entrance door to each carriage, and they order people to slow down.

We're almost there now. We're so close!

But just as I climb the steps to the carriage, with my mother holding onto me, one of the officers grabs my hand and pulls me back down to the platform.

"Follow me!" he says.

I can't believe our bad luck.

The officer leads the way to a closed room in the station.

I tell myself to stay calm. But when I look back at my mother trailing behind me, her face is as white as a sheet, and I'm worried she's going to faint.

I enter the official-looking room. Mama remains standing near the door.

"My mother has a heart condition," I tell the officer. "She needs some rest and a drink of water."

To my surprise, the officer fetches her a glass of water and brings her a chair. I guess he doesn't want to deal with someone having a heart attack on his shift.

He checks our documents. I make sure he can see the Komsomol card I qualified for at school. It means that I belong to the Young Communist League. I can tell it makes an impression on him.

He gives me back the documents and begins to ask me questions. Like everyone else in Stalin's Soviet Union, I'm used to answering questions.

Then he asks me to open the suitcases.

He rummages through our belongings.

I realize he's looking for contraband—state goods that people often steal, like faucets, pipes, thermometers and so on.

My heart stops when he picks up the loudspeaker, with its loose wires and homemade switch. I realize that I don't actually know where Yuri found it.

"What's this?" he asks sternly.

"It was for a school project on electricity," I say. I have no idea how that lie came to me so fast. I guess my brain works extra hard when it's a matter of life and death. "I got second prize," I continue, to add realism.

I don't know if he believes me, but he shakes the loudspeaker and decides that nothing could possibly be hidden inside it and that it's too pathetic to be state property.

He looks sharply at me, then at Mama, then back at me.

Our fate is the hands of this unknown, random person. He can decide to arrest us. He doesn't need a reason. He can make one up. If Mama's arrested again, she might not survive. And everyone who helped her could be in trouble, too.

Or he can let us go.

Which will it be?

I sense he knows that he has the power, right at this minute, to change our lives forever. He can destroy us or save us.

How can one person—a complete stranger— have so much power?

I'm afraid to look at Mama, afraid almost to breathe. I can hear a clock ticking somewhere. *Tick-tock, tick-tock.*

"Fine, you may go."

I grab the suitcases and lead Mama back to the train. I force myself not to run, so as not to appear guilty.

Maybe he liked us. Maybe he looked into our eyes and decided that he didn't want to ruin our lives.

Or maybe he couldn't be bothered.

Whatever the reason, it's nothing but sheer luck.

I'm sure we've missed our chance with the train. So I pull out one of the three cigarette packs I brought for bribes, and as we approach the train door, I slip them into the conductor's hand. He steps aside and lets us in.

There are no seats left, but we've made it. We're on a train to Novosibirsk.

A real train. A train for humans. We're one step closer to seeing Papa.

We even have a place to stay in Novosibirsk while we wait for a train to Moscow.

We find a spot at the end of the crowded aisle and sit down on our suitcases.

"The good thing is that he didn't see anything suspicious in our documents," I tell my mother. "Now we know for sure they're okay. And in a few hours, we'll be in Novosibirsk!"

It's too late to knock on Olga and Peter's door by the time we reach Novosibirsk, but the train station, the one that looks like a palace, is so enormous that we can sleep on the floor of the waiting hall.

But when we wake up at dawn, my mother slides her hand inside her shirt and gives a dreadful shriek.

All her money is gone.

5

Gray Eyes

Mama was so careful. She only removed money from her shirt in the bathroom stalls, even though the station's bathrooms are so vile you can faint just walking past the door. Whenever someone goes in or out, a smell like the pits of hell blasts out at you.

But a sharp-eyed thief must have seen my mother holding her collar, and maybe tapping her shirt to make sure the money was still there.

And while we were both asleep, the thief reached in and stole it.

My mother begins to wail like a child. It's a bit embarrassing.

"We still have the other half in my boots," I tell her.

But she shakes her head. She must be thinking about how hard she worked for every kopek, knitting for hours and hours, week after week, month after month. And about what risks poor Papa must have taken to send us money.

But the truly disastrous part is that we won't be

able to get to Moscow, where Papa will be waiting for us.

Suddenly I remember. I still have Felicia's emerald earrings!

Not that I forgot. It's just that I got so used to saving my treasure for an emergency that I stopped thinking about it.

I lean over and whisper in my mother's ear, "I still have Felicia's earrings in the seam of my coat."

My mother stops crying and looks at me with surprise. "I was sure they were gone by now!" she exclaims.

"You told me to hold on to them, and I did."

A proud smile spreads over my mother's face. "My darling son. You are the clever knight who comes to the rescue."

We fill our mugs with boiling water, wait until the water cools and do our best to wash our faces and comb our hair. We still look rumpled and dusty and patched-up, but then so do most of the people around us.

We walk with our suitcases to the schoolyard — the one where we stayed for a week when we first arrived in Siberia.

Today is Saturday, and the yard is deserted.

The memory of our first day here comes rushing back to me. A straggling group of refugees, dazed and weak, miraculously still alive. Our joy at finding a water tap, at getting clean inside the banya, at being out in the open air. Felicia's escape in the middle of the night. Andreas being called away to work for the war effort.

I didn't have any idea what was waiting for us. No one did.

We climb in through the log fence, drink from the wall tap, wash our hands and make one last effort to look as clean and presentable as possible.

Then we pick up our suitcases and head for Reka Street.

Even though we're walking slowly, my heart starts to beat like a thundering drum in my chest.

All this time, trying to be invisible, trying to be a nobody—I suddenly feel as if I really have turned into a nobody. What if the smell from the vile bathrooms at the station has rubbed off on me? What if I'm not just a nobody, but a disgusting, stinky nobody?

For the first time in my life I'm ashamed not only of myself, but also of Mama. She used to be so pretty, with her rosy cheeks and happy smile and sparkling eyes. She wore nice clothes and was elegant all round.

Now she looks droopy and old. Her shoes are falling apart and her coat looks like it's been through an earthquake followed by a shipwreck followed by a tornado.

I'm no better. Even the chocolate bar that I was so

excited about giving to Olga is probably contaminated by the bad smell now. The thought of the ruined chocolate depresses me even more than the theft of our money.

The closer we get to Reka Street, the more gloomy I become, and the more convinced that I reek to the high heavens. I want to turn around and go back. I really think I would, if I were alone. I really think I'd rather sleep in the train station, or maybe die, than show up right now at Olga and Peter's doorstep.

Number 17 is a big house, but we can't tell how many people live inside — whether one family or ten.

There's a piece of tape on the doorbell, with the word *BROKEN* scrawled on it. Me and the doorbell, I think.

We use the knocker instead. I feel so awful I think I might vomit right here on the doorstep.

A beautiful gray-eyed teenager wearing a short dance skirt, white tights and pink ballet slippers opens the door.

My heart stops pounding like a wild drum. Instead, it nearly stops beating altogether.

Olga has changed since I last saw her, changed a lot, but I'd know her anywhere.

She recognizes me, too. "Natt! Is this your mother? Hello, Mrs. Sil — I mean, Mrs. Sokolov. Do come in. Lovely to meet you."

I try to keep my distance from Olga, because I'm

now completely sure that I smell of the station toilets. When Olga shows us into the living room, I make a beeline for the window seat and pray that I'm far enough for the bad-smell molecules to be dispersed in the air. Luckily, the window is slightly open.

Olga isn't like anyone I know. Neither is Peter, when he joins us.

They love to joke and clown about, and they say whatever pops into their heads.

My mother likes them instantly, I can tell.

"So kind of you to welcome us," she says. She's fluent in Russian, of course, but she still has a German accent.

"Oh, I love your European accent!" Olga says. "Wait till Father hears it. He'll have a million questions about your ancestors. He's at work. He works all hours. And Mother is away, who knows where! Cousin Frieda will make us tea."

She vanishes into another room. I take a look around me. The furniture is worn and plain, and the stuffing is coming out of the torn sofa cushions, but the walls are covered with the most beautiful paintings I've ever seen. You can see every detail of every person and object, even the tiny creases in their clothes and the varnish on furniture, but at the same time it all looks like someone's dream.

One of the paintings is of Lenin, as usual, but it's not a Lenin I've ever seen. He's looking out the window at a white owl perched on a snow-covered branch with bright red berries.

It's overwhelming to be surrounded by such wonderful art, but what's really overwhelming is being in the same house as Olga.

Because, no question about it, I am madly, desperately, head over heels in love with Olga.

I know it's a hopeless love. I know that someone like Olga would never be interested in a smelly, dusty, semi-invisible exile.

But I can't help myself.

6

A Dream of Dancers

A tall woman wearing some kind of Spanish costume enters the room carrying a tray. On the tray are two glasses of tea and two slices of black bread with jam.

Olga skips in behind her.

"Cousin Frieda's an actress," Olga says, as if she's telling us a funny joke. "We have seven cousins living with us now." I'm guessing they're cousins the same way that I've been a nephew on several occasions.

Olga and Peter chatter away as we drink the sweet lemony tea. I haven't had such delicious tea in a long time, and I'm hoping the sweet lemon scent will help disguise my bad smell.

Olga tells us that she has to practice ballet for many hours each day, and that she has special permission to spend less time in school so she can study dance.

"I want to join the Bolshoi," she says with a laugh that makes me think of crystal wind chimes or a brook babbling in the forest. "Yes, I know. Every girl says that. Every girl in dance school wants to be the next Anna Pavlova. But I work harder than anyone and I keep winning prizes, so I think I really have a chance."

After tea, Olga disappears to "do some stretches," and Peter shows us around. I'll be sleeping on a cot at the end of the upstairs hallway, and Mama will be sharing a room with Cousin Nina, Cousin Lisa and Cousin Ludmilla.

"Cousin Ludmilla snores like a tractor. Sorry about that," Peter chuckles.

Our last stop is the shower room. "Not much hot water, unfortunately," he says. "But it's not ice-cold, either. Well, you probably want to unpack. Make yourselves at home. Everyone else does!"

I'm happy to have the time alone. I need to sort out my thoughts and my feelings. I also need to shower as soon as possible. I don't think I've ever been so desperate for a shower.

Mama lets me go first. I carefully remove the pouch with the (probably ruined) chocolate from around my neck and leave it on the cot.

I want to say a prayer of thanks for the bar of soap hanging in a string bag from a nail on the bathroom wall. I scrub myself and my hair until at last I feel clean. There's a small towel, also hanging from a nail. The towel is tattered at the edges and there are several small holes in the thin fabric. The holes in the towel make me feel better.

I dry myself and sniff my clothes to see which are the least disgusting.

Unfortunately, the least disgusting are also the most patched-up. But I can tell now that Olga and Peter won't mind. Not only because of the tattered towel. When Peter showed us around, I saw that Cousin Pasha and Cousin Solomon were just as scruffy as us.

Before I lie down on the cot, I unzip the pouch and lift it to my nose. What luck! It smells perfectly fine. Thanks to the invention of the zipper, Olga's chocolate bar has survived intact.

I lie down on the cot and shut my eyes. And drift into a happy dream filled with dancers and leaps in the air, and I find that if I spin my legs very fast, I can actually walk on air for minutes at a time. It's not hard. You just have to figure out how to do it.

"Darling, it's suppertime." My mother is shaking my shoulder to wake me. I've been asleep for hours.

Mama and I go downstairs. I can hear Olga's voice coming from the kitchen, along with a jumble of other unfamiliar voices.

We stop at the doorway to the kitchen. Inside, food is being haphazardly pulled out of the icebox, chopped, sliced, heated up. There's a huge pot of macaroni on the stove and another of soup. I count eight men and women along with Peter and Olga, and they all seem to be talking at once.

A man with messy hair and dark-framed glasses notices us and comes over to shake our hands. He's around Mama's age, and his clothes are even more crumpled and mended than hers, if that's possible.

"Cousins, dear cousins!" he calls out. "I would like to introduce you to Comrade Sophie and her son Natan. Or is it Natt? They are friends of my children and our very special guests, stopping with us on the way to Moscow. How very pleased I am to meet you. I've heard a lot about you, Natt, and your immense love of literature and the Periodic Table of Elements. I'm Comrade Edward. Help yourselves. As you can see, we're informal here."

Many of the cousins eat standing up or sitting on the stairs or even sitting cross-legged on the floor. But Olga and Peter tell us to bring our plates to the living room. Olga sits next to me on the sofa. She's only inches away from me. Her slender arm as she lifts the spoon to her mouth is the most exquisite thing I've ever seen in my life. I feel almost faint with happiness.

Mama and I soon find out that Comrade Edward is one of the nicest men in the world. As nice as Papa.

He tells us we can stay in his house as long as we need to. He tells us he will organize ration cards for us.

Then he says he has a friend, Viktor, who is traveling to Moscow in three or four weeks, and if we don't mind waiting that long, Viktor will take care of us.

"He'll make sure you get a berth in the soft section," he says.

It seems the train has a soft section and two hard sections, and the soft section is much, much better.

"Half our money was stolen at the station," Mama tells him. "We have a pair of valuable earrings to sell, but we're not sure how much we can get for them."

Comrade Edward looks shocked. "How dreadful! But don't worry. We'll help you sell the earrings. And we would all be grateful, Comrade Sophie, if you'd knit some warm clothes for the children and the cousins."

While their father speaks, Olga and Peter put on a hilarious mime show. Peter pretends he's a woman selling her earrings to a haughty shopkeeper (Olga), and the two of them begin to haggle vehemently over the price, and it's hard to tell whether we're smiling and then laughing because of the miraculous things their father is telling us or because of the funny performance.

When we finish eating, Olga puts Schubert's beautiful *Serenade* on the gramophone and performs for us in the living room.

She dances like a real ballerina

She's so perfect it's hard to breathe.

Can this be real, or is it a dream? I really could be walking on air, the way I feel now.

7

Like a Shoe

When the recital is over, Olga glides over to the sofa and takes my hand.

"Come see our photos, Natt."

Peter begins to follow us, but she shoos him away. "*Kysh*, Petiaka! Natt and I have some private things to discuss."

Her words send a shiver down my spine.

She shows me to a little sewing and storage room just off the kitchen and pulls a large black photo album from a shelf that's crammed with albums, leaflets and documents tied up in string.

The photos are mostly of her relatives from long ago, and she tells me stories about each one. But my mind keeps wandering. All I can think about is how painful it is to be in love. I didn't know it actually hurts.

A second album has postcards from around the world.

"I want to travel," Olga says. "I want to see everything. Italy, France, England, Switzerland…

That's why I want to be in the Bolshoi. I'd be ecstatic just to be in the corps—that's the group dancers."

I understand. No one is allowed to leave the Soviet Union. Not really. Not without special permission, which is almost impossible to get.

But the Bolshoi Ballet toured all over the world before the war. I'm sure they'll continue once the war is over.

And it looks as if the war really will be over very soon. Hitler is finished. Everyone is saying he should surrender, because he doesn't have a chance, but he refuses to face reality.

"Hold on," I say.

I can't wait a minute longer to give Olga my gift, but I'm afraid that if I leave the room, she'll leave, too, and the wonderful moment will end. So I add, "Don't move. I'll be right back. I have something for you."

I dash upstairs, grab my zippered pouch and return to the storage room. Luckily, Olga is still there, leafing through the albums.

"I brought you a present," I say.

I unzip the pouch and hand her the wrapped bar.

"Chocolate! How did you know? Oh, wait, I remember! When we first met, at the school—I asked if you had any chocolate," she says, laughing her babbling-brook laugh. "What a nincompoop I was! But how did you find it?"

"I got lucky…"

"You're so sweet, Natt. We'll have to share it three ways. You, me, Peter…"

"Oh, no, I don't want any," I tell her. "I had lots in Tomsk."

Which is not a complete lie, because when I tutored Gennady, his mother used to give us one "chocolate cookie" each. But it wasn't really a cookie and it didn't really have chocolate in it. It was more like eating bitter sand.

"I once had Swiss chocolate," Olga explains. "Before the war. My mother bought it from a tourist in Moscow. It was the best thing I'd ever tasted."

"I have a friend in Switzerland," I say. "Max. But I haven't heard from him in a long time. I don't think he got my letters."

"*Comme c'est triste!*" Olga exclaims. That's another thing she likes to do—say things in French. French is her second language after Russian.

We compare the languages we know. We talk about our favorite words, our favorite music, our favorite fun times.

Then suddenly she leans over and kisses my nose. "You're sweet, Natt," she repeats. "I like you. Maybe next week after my ballet class we'll all go see a movie or a show. Father always finds things to see. How old are you, by the way?"

"I turned fifteen two weeks ago, on April 1st."

"April Fool's Day, how funny!"

"What about you?"

"I turned fourteen in December," she says. "You must be exhausted, sleeping in the train station, and that long ride from Tomsk."

Hard to believe it was only yesterday. My whole life has been transformed since then.

"I slept all afternoon," I say. "Besides, I'm used to sleeping in strange places. I've slept in so many places I can't even count them."

"Oh, tell me!" Olga says, closing the postcard album and hugging it. I wish I was that album.

I begin to tell her about the gym in Czernowitz and how on our last day there, the Germans began to drop bombs on the city. Then the so-called bunk on the so-called train, the courtyard in Novosibirsk—

"Just round the corner," she interrupts.

I nod and continue. The barge under the pouring rain. The Community House in the middle of nowhere. The three-to-a-bed in the kitchen. The room in Bakchar with Irena before she left, the straw bed at the Mindrus', the government inn with Mr. Wilmer, the various floors and shared beds during the sleigh ride, the hospital, the platform that hung from the ceiling. I don't mention Dr. Sima, and of course I don't mention the reason Mama and I were separated for a year.

Olga listens with wide eyes.

"It's like something out of a novel," she says. "So

many adventures and misadventures…and all my life I've only lived in this one house. Let's have some chocolate."

She tries to break off a piece of chocolate but it's not easy. The bar is unusually hard. We both try, and finally, after many efforts, we succeed.

Olga pops the piece in her mouth, makes a hilariously surprised face, yelps like a puppy and spits it out into her hand.

"This tastes like a shoe," she says, laughing.

I'm mortified. How unlucky can a person be? I feel like crying.

I break off a second piece and take a nibble. The chocolate is truly revolting. "Like a shoe a rat died in," I say.

This makes Olga laugh even harder, and I can't help smiling. "A shoe a rat died in after puking," Olga just manages to say between uncontrollable howls.

"A shoe…a shoe…" I'm now laughing my head off, too, and I can barely get the words out. "A shoe a rat died in after puking in a dungeon."

"Dur…dur…during the French Revolution!" Olga sputters.

We're now laughing so hard that tears roll down Olga's cheeks, and my stomach starts to hurt.

Eventually we calm down. "I'll bet you my father will eat it," Olga says. "He'd eat anything rather than throw out food."

We talk until past midnight. I find out more about the cousins, who are all musicians, writers or other kinds of artists — "all of them staunch members of the Party," Olga laughs.

In other words, they are safe, at least for now.

But that's the only time she mentions politics or the Soviet Union, apart from telling me that her mother is involved in "the war effort" and her father does "research for the government."

She doesn't ask about my father. We both know there are some things that even the best of friends had better not talk about. Not while Stalin is in charge.

Olga will never love me, but at least she likes me. It's better than nothing.

And she kissed my nose.

8

Not a Ghost

I lie down in my cot and shut my eyes. I try to hold on to the image of Olga leaning forward to kiss my nose.

But instead I find myself thinking of Lucy, the dentist's daughter in Zastavna.

Lucy lived across the street from us. Her mother was in a sanitarium and she was an only child, so she often spent the evenings at our place. We played checkers (she usually won) and card games. She always smelled of sweet lavender, because her uncle in Budapest owned a soap factory, and he used to send her scented soap.

Then the Russians took over our town, and instead of separate classes for boys and girls, we were all in the same classroom. Suddenly Lucy was sitting next to me at school.

I began to look forward to the lavender smell and to miss it when she was absent. And I began to notice more things about her. The way she added flowery decorations to her letters. The way she held her pen.

Her cute little ears and shy smile.

Why am I thinking of Lucy when I'm in love with Olga?

Because just before we were exiled, Lucy made me a card with a heart and butterflies. I kept it in my inside jacket pocket all through the train ride to Siberia, but it got ruined on the barge when we were trapped in the pouring rain.

I never had a chance to say goodbye to her. One day, just like that, she was gone. On the train to Siberia, Andreas the Tall told me that she went to live with her uncle in Budapest. The one who owned the soap factory.

I want to think only about Olga, but as I slip into sleep, Olga and Lucy become one person, and I'm both happy and sad, because I don't know if Olga/Lucy is real or just a figment of my imagination.

When I wake up, I'm back to being thrilled about Olga. I've left Lucy behind in my dream and she fades as the dream fades.

"I know someone who comes from your town," Comrade Edward tells me and Mama at breakfast. Breakfast is as chaotic as supper was the day before. People just grab what they can and then eat in their corner. Cousin Frieda hands me a slice of bread and a bowl of leftover soup.

Olga has already left for school. I'll be counting the minutes until she comes back.

"Is it Andreas Loeffler by any chance?" Mama asks.

"Yes! How did you know?"

Mama tells him how Andreas the Tall was called away just before we left the courtyard. She doesn't mention his terror, or how relieved he was when he found out he wasn't being arrested.

"A lovely man! How is he doing?" she asks.

"I'll invite him to the show tonight, and you can see for yourself."

"What show?" I ask. "Is Olga in it?"

Comrade Edward smiles. "No, it's a local variety show with some of our city's most talented performers."

I spend the day waiting to be asked to do chores. It feels strange not to have to fetch pails of water or chop wood.

But no one expects me to work. Mama knits, and I look for a book to read to her.

"Something funny, if you can find it," she says.

I ask Cousin Solomon for a funny novel and he gives me *The Twelve Chairs*. Mama enjoys it, but I can barely concentrate on what I'm reading. I keep looking at the clock.

Olga finally comes home just minutes before we have to leave for the show. In the commotion of everyone getting ready I barely have a chance to say hello, and I suddenly feel shy and awkward. She's so lively and confident, and I've been a ghost for so long that I begin to wonder if she's forgotten all about me.

The theater is just a big room with a makeshift stage and folding chairs. It's easy to spot Andreas the Tall towering over the crowd. He comes over and gives me a big hug. There are tears in his eyes.

"*How do you do*," I say in English. I don't know if he even remembers giving me the English primer. "*It's a fine day today.*"

He laughs. "Very good, Natt. What a relief it is to see the two of you," he says, kissing Mama and resting his hands on my shoulders. "I hope things have been…" he trails off. "I hear you're on your way to Moscow. Before you go, you must come over for supper and meet my wife. Yes, I'm married now."

The lights flash, and we all take our seats. Mine is between Olga and Peter.

The show begins.

It is without doubt the worst show in the history of human shows, with one terrible performance after another.

Two boys play the balalaika horribly.

An old woman comes on stage and croaks out a poem about Lenin and Stalin called "Final Conflagration." It's set to music, but the gramophone isn't working properly and the music is mostly crackles, buzzing and a strange high-pitched squeak. She pretends not to notice.

A juggler on a unicycle juggles six rings pretty impressively until he begins to cough and has to ride off the stage, clutching the rings to his chest.

Several people with wreaths of paper flowers on their heads dance in a circle. Their flowers keep slipping and covering half their faces, which makes them stumble into one another because they can't see properly.

The worse the performance is, the more Peter and Olga cheer, whistle, clap and shout "Bravo!" I join in and before long we're drowning in a fit of helpless giggles.

As we all walk home, Olga and I lag behind the others. Olga takes my hand in hers. We laugh again at the terrible show.

Suddenly Olga says, "Do you love me?"

Without pausing to think about whether I should admit it or not, I blurt out, "Yes," and then wonder if I've been a fool.

But it's the right answer.

"I love you, too," she says. "You're smart, you're cute, and you're not angry about your bad luck. You're actually the most interesting person I've ever met."

I want to think of something clever to say, but my mind goes blank just when I need it most!

But Olga continues to chat away, and I don't have to say anything more.

I'm not a ghost after all.

I'm interesting.

9

Olga Loves a Mystery

Knowing that Olga loves me makes me happier than I've ever been in my life. I feel like the luckiest person on the planet.

At the same time, I can't help worrying about Mama and about our situation, especially while Olga's at school.

1. Mama knits all day, hoping to pay Comrade Edward back for his kindness. Everyone in the house has asked for something—scarf, mitts, long johns, sweaters. If Mama works from morning to night, she can finish a sweater in two and a half days. I'm worried about how hard she's working, but I'm also worried she won't be able to fill everyone's orders.

2. There hasn't been any word from Papa. Will he make it to Moscow? How will we arrange to meet him?

3. Will Comrade Edward find a buyer for the emerald earrings, and if so, how much will we get for them? Will it be enough?

There's nothing I can do about any of these things.

Instead, I try to help around the house. I've washed all the floors and windows. I've scrubbed the bathroom, tidied the linen chest and helped Solomon clean his paintbrushes. (He's the artist who painted all the beautiful pictures in the house. He's engaged to Ludmilla, who plays the violin in an orchestra. Nina, Ludmilla's sister, plays the flute.)

I've helped Frieda rehearse her lines for a play about barley, and I spent an entire day filing Pasha's notes for a book he's writing about Cousin Solomon.

Finally a letter arrives from Sima.

Dear Sophie and Natt,

I hope you are well and enjoying your stay with your relatives in Novosibirsk. My good friend Sonya is looking forward to your arrival in Moscow on May 20th. She will meet you at 4:00 p.m. at Yaroslavsky Station. If your train is delayed, she will come the next day.

Do write soon!

Wishing you all the best,

Sima Israelovna, Member of the Communist Party

"Sonya" is Papa, of course. He's going to show up every day at 4:00 p.m. at the Moscow train station, starting on May 20th, until we arrive.

I can't believe I'll actually be seeing Papa in six weeks. I'm feeling a little confused about it, actually.

A little nervous. I don't know why. I can't explain it.

I wish I could talk to Olga about how I feel, but no one can know the truth. Olga's father could get into terrible trouble for giving aid to refugees with false papers. He could lose everything, and maybe even go to prison.

The little storeroom off the kitchen has become our private meeting place. Peter likes to tease us by calling it our love lair. Olga has let the whole house know how we feel about each other, and that means she isn't ashamed of loving me.

Everyone is happy for us, including Mama.

We're in our love lair now, playing mikado. You throw long thin sticks on a table and you have to pick them up one at a time without making the other sticks move. I never manage to get farther than three or four turns before the sticks move. Olga thinks my butterfingers are hilarious.

And right now my fingers are clumsier than ever, because I'm distracted. I'm thinking about Papa and wishing I could talk to Olga about how I feel.

Suddenly I get an idea.

I can tell Olga about Papa without revealing that he was ever in the Gulag. When I asked Olga and Peter for help, I said that my father had been wounded while fighting in the Red Army. Why not talk about my feelings without changing that part of the story?

I won't lie. I'll just leave out a few details.

"Olga," I begin, gathering the sticks after losing yet again, "can I ask you something?"

"Oh, that sounds mysterious! I love a mystery!"

"It's about meeting my papa. I feel…a little…I don't know how I feel. I mean, I'm so happy! I haven't seen him in more than three years, but at the same time…I don't know how to explain it…"

"You can stop right there," Olga says, and for a second I'm afraid that she's going to get angry at me for involving her in a risky topic.

But she continues, "I know exactly what you're talking about. My mother used to go away for months at a time. And once when I was around six, she'd been away for ages—it seemed like years to me, but it was probably around five months. And when she came back, I hated her. I wouldn't say hello, I wouldn't talk to her, I completely ignored her. I pretended she wasn't even there."

"Gosh," I say. I'm already starting to feel better.

"I was mad at her. I was giving her the message, *Fine—if you don't love me enough to be here, I don't need you.* Maybe I was even punishing her."

"Even though you knew it wasn't her fault," I say.

"That's right. I did know. I knew perfectly well, because she told me, and she wrote me letters about how much she missed me. She had an important job, and she couldn't say no even if she wanted to."

I nod. "Papa didn't have a choice, either."

"But we still get mad. Maybe we're just angry at life, and we let it out on them because they're supposed to be in charge."

"But there's something else," I say, wondering whether I should tell her, but unable to stop myself. "I did something really awful. Really, really awful. I guess I'm worried he hasn't forgiven me. And maybe I'm worried he'll be angry. You see..."

I try to think of a way to tell her about how I turned my head away when I walked by the jail, knowing he was at the window.

Olga waits patiently. It's as if she knows I'm looking for a way to tell her what happened without revealing too much.

"It was March 14th, three years ago. I had a chance to see him from a distance. Just this one time. And I..."

Suddenly I'm worried that Olga will be disgusted with me when I tell her. And won't love me anymore.

"You turned away from him?"

My eyes widen. Does Olga have mind-reading powers? How could she possibly have known?

She laughs. Her laugh always thrills me, even now that I've heard it so often.

"You're looking at me as if I'm a sorcerer. But it's just common sense. What's the point of seeing your parent from a distance when what you need is to have them there all the time? Better to pretend it's not happening at all."

"I was ashamed of him," I admit.

Olga lowers her eyes. She gets it now. She knows Papa wasn't a soldier at all. He was in prison. But she pretends she hasn't understood.

"Parents are so embarrassing," she says quickly, looking up at me. "Anyhow, believe me, he doesn't care. He's counting the minutes until he sees you and your mother. I can promise you he isn't mad at you. He's the one who feels guilty that he hasn't been there for you."

I sigh with relief. "I wish I was as smart as you," I say.

"I don't believe you, Mr. Periodic Table."

And we go back to playing mikado and talking about other things.

10

Daydreams in the Soft Section

I should be the happiest person on the planet right now.

Mama and I are on our way to see Papa. He's alive, he didn't die in the Gulag, he's meeting us in Moscow. After all this time we'll be a family again.

And we're leaving Siberia. For good. Maybe we'll even manage to leave the Soviet Union. We've heard that it's possible to leave the Soviet Union from Bucharest, if we can manage to get there. And there's a good chance we can. Papa has papers permitting him to "return" to Bucharest.

Once we're free, we can join our relatives in Canada. That was the plan five years ago, before the war.

We'll need more money. We didn't get as much as we'd hoped for the emerald earrings, because people are more interested in food than jewelry these days. The earrings paid for our train tickets to Moscow and food for the trip, but there's not much left.

Mama tells me not to worry. She says we'll find a way to return to Zastavna and dig up the money that we buried in our yard when the Russians came. She has a plan, but she hasn't told me what it is.

Meanwhile, not only are we on the train to Moscow, we're traveling in the soft section, thanks to Olga's father and his friend Viktor.

In the soft section you have your own compartment and a door you can lock. It's a bit hard to go in and out because of all the passengers in the corridor, and it's a bit stuffy because if you open the window, dust flies in. But you get a soft bed with a clean sheet and a pillow that's as hard as rock but who cares? It's better than using your boots!

Viktor is taking wonderful care of us. He has smiley eyes, a small white beard and a cane that I think is mostly for decoration. He showed me a new word game that's become popular. It's called a crossword puzzle. Viktor comes up with the puzzles and I solve them. It helps the time pass faster.

I love lying on the bed as the train chugs along. Until now, traveling through Siberia has been a misery, but for once I can actually enjoy the ride, and so can Mama. The view out the window, Russia in spring, makes me want to write a poem.

A poem for Olga, of course. Comparing how I feel about her to the landscape.

Unfortunately, or maybe fortunately, I'm not a poet.

Olga is the reason I'm not as happy as I should be. In fact, my heart is sort of breaking. When will I see her again? How will I see her? How can she leave the USSR, and even if she could, would she want to leave her family and everything she knows?

I go over everything that happened in Novosibirsk. We kissed four times.

We went to a hotel restaurant for a belated celebration of my birthday. It took three hours for the dessert we ordered (tinned apricots covered with soggy cookie crumbs) to arrive. That suited me just fine.

We went to a movie and held hands.

We went to two music concerts. Cousin Ludmilla and Cousin Nina were in the orchestra.

Olga taught me French, which will come in useful if we join our relatives in Montreal. She said I'm a very fast learner. French is now my eighth language, if you count English.

I read a book Olga gave me. It's her favorite book. It's called *Little Women*, and I have to admit I liked it.

We celebrated the marriage of Cousin Ludmilla and Cousin Solomon, which took place in an office, but when they came home we had a party for them. Then they had a big fight about whether wearing a wedding band is a sign of loyalty and devotion (Ludmilla) or a sign of female slavery (Solomon). Peter and Olga, as always, acted the fight out behind their backs with exaggerated mime, which made everyone laugh hysterically.

Olga showed me how to play a string game where

you make a pattern of string with your hands and pass it from person to person, making new patterns, like carpet, field, fish.

I watched her practice ballet.

We went for walks. We worked in the garden. We saw the stars at night. In Siberia nights are pitch black, and you can see a million stars once the sun sets.

I go over everything in my mind again and again, and then I daydream. Olga is accepted to the Bolshoi. We end up in Canada, and then the Bolshoi comes to perform there…and Olga decides to stay…

These memories and daydreams keep me company all day long and all night long.

After two weeks of daydreaming about Olga and then night-dreaming about Olga, so that I'm half-asleep when I'm awake and half-awake when I'm asleep, word spreads down the train that we're one day away from Moscow.

11

The Moscow Station

Mama looks more like she used to before Siberia. Her eyes are shining again and her frown isn't as deep. The long train ride—with nothing for her to do but catch up on years of lost sleep—has restored her.

It's early dawn when the train finally pulls into the station. Viktor wants us to go with him to his hotel, but we explain that "someone" is coming to meet us, and that we absolutely can't leave the station.

He writes down his hotel address just in case and disappears into the crowd. I'll probably never see him again. One more person I'm leaving behind, maybe forever. Such a long list by now.

Now we have to wait until 4:00 p.m.

The hours crawl by. I'm restless and impatient and excited. I try to reread *Little Women* or solve one of Viktor's crossword puzzles, but I can't concentrate. I'm finding it hard not to pace up and down the station. But of course I mustn't call attention to myself.

Mama, on the other hand, is as still as a statue. It's

almost as if she's afraid to be too happy in case Papa doesn't show up. Because in Stalin's Russia, you never know what will happen, and very often the worst possible thing happens. Papa could show up to meet us, or he could be in trouble again.

But when trouble does come, it comes to us, not to Papa.

My mistake was to pick up a newspaper that someone left on a bench. The news is good. Hitler is getting slaughtered by the Allies. He's getting pounded from every side, and the Americans especially are giving it to him good. His situation is hopeless. He's losing battle after battle. The war will be over any day. He just has to surrender.

I smile with relief as I read.

A police guard sees me smiling and marches over to our bench. "You two! Follow me! At once!"

His voice makes my blood run cold. It's the tone guards use just before they arrest you.

He thinks I was laughing at Stalin, or at an article about how great the Soviet Union is.

I feel sick as we follow him with our suitcases. Mama tries to take my hand but I shake it off. I don't know why.

The guard leads us to a small, dark, windowless room and locks the door. We're sitting there, just the two of us on the one bench.

Detained.

Or imprisoned. That's what a locked door means.

We know better than to say a word to one another. The room is for sure bugged.

After a very long time — I don't know how long, but it feels like hours — another guard enters. His eyes are like blue pools of ice. I can feel Mama trembling next to me and trying to control her breathing.

"You first," he says to me, and I leave Mama in the little room. I follow the guard into a bare office with a desk. He sits behind the desk and I remain standing.

"Sit!" he barks at me, as if it were a swear word.

I sit down and pray that the reference letter from Mrs. Gordeev will help us. It's in my inside jacket pocket.

Suddenly I panic. What if it got wet and the ink ran? What if it got torn? I haven't looked at it since we left Novosibirsk.

"Where are you coming from? Speak up!" he growls, as if I've already spoken and my voice wasn't loud enough.

I tell him the story we planned on the train.

"My mother and I were in Tomsk, waiting for my father, who was in the Red Army. But we got word that he was wounded and he asked us to come to Moscow. Just before we left, we found out that he died. We're now waiting for our friend Viktor. He will arrange for me to continue my studies here. I was top in my class in Tomsk. I even tutored."

I reach inside my jacket pocket and retrieve the letter. I hand it to him, folded.

He opens it, and I'm relieved to see that it's still in one piece, just a bit creased.

His face doesn't change as he reads. His eyes are as ice-blue as ever.

But he's taking his time. He's pretending to read while he decides what to do. At this point he's had enough time to memorize it.

"Wait here!" he orders, and he leaves the room with the letter.

I wait for a long time.

What if he has a quota, and he needs to round up two more people today? In that case, the letter will stand in his way and he'll want to get rid of it.

But when he returns he's still holding the letter. He gives it back to me.

"So you worked for Colonel Gordeev, did you?" he asks. He's trying to sound as angry as before, but I can tell his heart is no longer in it.

"Yes, sir. I tutored his son, Gennady. A very smart boy."

"At what address?"

I give him the address, even though it's at the top of the letter.

"And what subjects did you tutor him in?"

"All the subjects. Russian literature, math, history, biology, chemistry."

"And what were you laughing at in the newspaper?"

"I was so happy to read that we're defeating Hitler. He has to surrender! We won."

He suddenly seems depressed, and he waves his arm at me. The wave seems to mean that I can go, but I'm not sure, so I remain in my chair.

"I said you can go! And don't dawdle here. I want you out of the station, you and your mother. Wait for your friend somewhere else. This is a train station, not a library. Scram!"

I couldn't be more relieved to be told to scram. I remember all the words for "exiled" that I came up with on the train to Siberia. I never thought I'd be so happy to hear one of them.

When my mother sees me, she jumps up from the bench. She looks pale and terrified.

I take her arm and lead her out to the corridor.

"Everything is fine," I whisper. "We have to leave the station." As if we'd want to stay after that!

"Thank God," she mumbles. "And all the good angels, and anyone else who's in charge."

It's 3:15 p.m.

We quickly leave the station and look around for a way to blend into the crowds and not be noticed.

In fact, the crowds are suddenly very heavy. A train has just arrived, and passengers are pouring in and out of the station.

I look around, trying to decide which way to go.

But even though it's early, I suddenly see a bearded figure in a long coat standing under the spire, his eyes hidden by a hat. He seems to be waiting for someone.

Can it be?

No, it must be someone else. Papa is taller, and he doesn't have a beard.

But something about the way he's standing and looking around...something about him...

A second later, my mother sees him, too. She gasps and clutches my arm.

That's how I know. She wouldn't get it wrong.

Everyone else becomes invisible.

They're the ones who are ghosts now. All I can see is Papa.

I run into his arms.

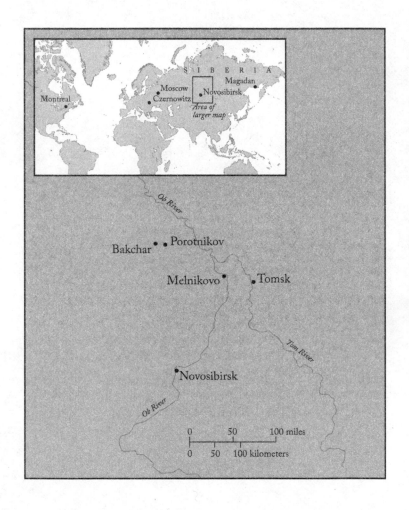

Author's Note

Dear Reader,

A Boy Is Not a Ghost is based on the childhood experiences of my fifth-grade teacher, Nahum Halpern. Every Friday, Nahum told us amazing stories from his past. I wrote *A Boy Is Not a Bird* and *A Boy Is Not a Ghost* so that others could enjoy those stories. Nahum emerged from his difficult years in Siberia with a philosophy of life that he shared with us and modeled every day: *Be kind, do the right thing, consider others, and enjoy the funny and fantastic and weird things in life. Don't let anyone be an outsider. We all belong together.*

Nahum gave me permission to add characters and fictional events to the true story of his life. But every challenge that Natt experiences in Siberia is taken from real life, including the barge, winter in Porotnikov and his mother's imprisonment (in reality she was jailed for three years), his father's years in the Gulag, Natt's guilt at turning his head away, Irena's departure, his time with the Mindrus, the sleigh ride and Natt's hospital stay, the buried treasure in Zastavna, ingenious Yuri (and his home improvements), Nadeja Michailovna, kind Sima Israelovna, the two NKVD officers and their sons, the escape and family reunion.

I hope you enjoy reading about Natt's incredible journey.

Yours,

Edeet

Historical Background

Rule of the Czars*

For centuries Russia was ruled by emperors known as czars. Like kings and queens, czars inherited their titles.

By 1900, Russia was the largest country in the world, and it had an estimated population of 100 million. But Russia was not as industrialized as Western Europe. Most Russians were illiterate peasant farmers who were still using the same farming methods their ancestors had used in the Middle Ages.

The czars were autocratic rulers, which meant that they alone had the power to lay down the law. They claimed that this power had been given to them by God. Their wealthy friends and associates, who made up about 10 percent of the population, owned all the land and were in charge of the army and the administration of the country. The czars appointed and paid these officials. In order to keep their positions, they had to be absolutely loyal to the czar and carry out his every instruction.

Laws were designed to keep the czar in power and punish anyone who questioned his authority. The punishment was usually exile to faraway Siberia. The czar called anyone who challenged him an "enemy of the state." Thousands of "enemies of the state" were banished to Siberia.

There was no elected government, and there were no

*Also called Tsars

courts of law that were not controlled by the czar. Books and newspapers were heavily censored, and it was a crime to read any writing that was critical of the state.

The czars ran a large network of secret police to root out suspicious behavior and crush anyone who opposed the regime. The police worked undercover, and their methods of silencing people were brutal. Virtually everyone was terrified of them.

In addition to secret police, the czars employed large armies to enforce their authority.

Rebellion

Since the czars refused to reform the legal system and improve living conditions for ordinary Russians, their opponents decided that the only way to bring about change was through revolution. Other countries in Western Europe had set up constitutional governments that gave citizens more rights. Opposition groups in Russia wanted the same rights, but the last czar of Russia, Nicholas II, refused to give up his power.

Russian revolutionary movements were inspired by the ideas of Karl Marx. Marx and Friedrich Engels published *The Communist Manifesto* in 1848. Marx predicted that working classes would not put up with injustice forever. They would liberate themselves from the control of the ruling classes. Once this was achieved, a socialist society based on equality for all could be established.

In 1917, Czar Nicholas II was overthrown by the Bolsheviks, a revolutionary party headed by Vladimir Lenin.

Lenin gave Joseph Stalin a top position in the new Communist Party, even though Stalin had already shown himself to be ruthless and bloodthirsty. In 1922, Russia became the Soviet Union (USSR). Two years later, Lenin died. On his deathbed, he left instructions about who should lead the party. Definitely not Stalin, he said. He was too dangerous.

Stalin was furious. No one was going to tell him what he could and could not do, and after Lenin died, he installed himself as dictator of the Soviet Union.

A Tragic Time

Stalin's years in power brought unimaginable suffering to millions of people. After Lenin's death, he "purged" the government and the military by killing or jailing politicians and generals he suspected of disloyalty. Applying the methods of the czars, he used the term "enemy of the people" to create a criminal category. Anyone could be imprisoned and even executed for this "crime."

Stalin's secret police, the NKVD, randomly arrested ordinary people (like Nahum Halpern's father) and sent them to labor prisons (all prisoners were required to do hard labor) or to distant forced labor camps known as Gulags. If you stole a loaf of bread, or didn't show up to work because you were sick, or told a joke that was critical of Stalin, or if someone said you weren't loyal, you could be executed or sent to the Gulag. People were encouraged to inform on one another, and children were asked to inform on their parents.

Officers of the NKVD were given quotas for the number of people they needed to arrest or kill. During the twenty-five years that Stalin was in charge, more than ten million people lost their lives. Some were executed, some died in a famine Stalin created, and some were sent to the Gulags, where most prisoners died of cold, illness and starvation—or at the hands of cruel guards. Millions of children became orphans.

Cult of Personality

Stalin did not want people to know what he was really like. So he lied about nearly everything, and he succeeded in making millions of people believe his lies. He did not allow the media to print anything negative about him. A political cartoon or a critical comment would get you imprisoned or killed. History books were rewritten with the facts altered to make Stalin look good. Older history books were destroyed or hidden away. It was illegal to own a book that had not been approved by Stalin.

Stalin used propaganda to convince people that he was a kind, caring, wonderful person who was saving Russia. He created a "cult of personality" or public image to manipulate people. He presented himself as a hero who was loved by Russians and, indeed, many people believed his lies and worshipped him. There were photos and posters of Stalin everywhere. In all of them he looked wise and fatherly. Schoolchildren became Young Pioneers and were taught to chant, "Thank you, Comrade Stalin, for our happy childhood."

World War II

In 1939, Adolf Hitler, the leader of Nazi Germany, tricked Stalin. Let me invade Poland (a country located between Germany and Russia), Hitler said, and in return we'll divide up the conquered land and I won't attack you. Stalin believed Hitler and agreed to the deal. The two countries signed a "nonaggression pact."

Once Stalin was in charge of the new territories, he deported hundreds of thousands of people from those territories to Siberia.

Then, on June 22, 1941 (while Nahum huddled with his mother in a gym, waiting to be sent to Siberia), everything changed. Hitler broke his promise and attacked Russia.

After six months of desperate battles, the United States entered the war. The US and the Soviet Union, along with Great Britain, Canada and other countries, fought together to defeat Hitler. British, Canadian and American soldiers attacked the German army from the west, and the Red Army attacked from the east. The German army was driven out of the Soviet Union. In early May 1945, the war in Europe was over.

After World War II

After the war, Stalin became more brutal than ever. The people of the Soviet Union, which now included all of Eastern Europe, were again terrorized by the NKVD. In the last year of his life, Stalin turned against Soviet Jews. Thousands of Jews were fired from their jobs and deported to Siberia. Stalin began to spread conspiracy lies about Jews and filled the newspapers with false stories and hatred. He murdered a group of thirteen Jewish poets. His next target was a group of doctors. But in 1953, a few weeks after he arrested the doctors, he died.

The dreadful years of Stalinism were over.

Acknowledgments

My deepest gratitude to
- ♥ Shelley Tanaka, my brilliant and endlessly patient Groundwood editor, who brought sparks and swirls to every page
- ♥ Karen Li for her faith, enthusiasm and always-kind support
- ♥ the marvelous Groundwood team
- ♥ Joan Deitch, whose boundless generosity was indispensable in the early stages of writing this book
- ♥♥♥♥♥♥♥ Luke, Larissa and Ivy, who are the center of my universe

In 1941, life in Natt's small town of Zastavna is comfortable and familiar. Natt knows there's a war on, of course, but he's glad their family didn't emigrate to Canada when they had a chance. He wouldn't want to leave his best friend, Max.

Then one day Natt goes home and finds his family huddled around the radio. The Russians are taking over. The churches and synagogues will close, Hebrew school will be held in secret, and there are tanks and soldiers in the street. But it's exciting, too. Natt wants to become a Young Pioneer, to show outstanding revolutionary spirit and make their new leader, Comrade Stalin, proud.

But life under the Russians is hard. And then Natt's father is arrested, and local authorities begin to round up deportees bound for Siberia.

- Canadian Jewish Literary Award, children/youth winner
- Sydney Taylor Book Award, middle-grade notable
- Silver Birch Award, fiction finalist
- Red Cedar Book Award, fiction nominee
- Vine Award for Canadian Jewish Literature, young adult/children's literature shortlist

"With a big heart and developing intellect, Natt is an endearing figure, and secondary characters are equally well drawn, especially his eternally optimistic mother."—*Publishers Weekly*

"Basing her story on the experience of a beloved teacher, Ravel has Natt tell his own story in an ingenuous present tense that never loses its youthful quality even as it gains wisdom…. An accessible gateway to mid-20th-century Eastern European history."—*Kirkus Reviews*

Edeet Ravel's young adult novel *Held* was nominated for the CLA Young Adult Book Award and the Arthur Ellis Crime Award. Her YA novel *The Saver* has been adapted for film and received awards around the globe. Her acclaimed novels for adults have won the Hugh MacLennan Prize and the Jewish Book Award and have been nominated for the Governor General's Award and the Giller Prize.

Edeet was born on an Israeli kibbutz and has a PhD in Jewish Studies from McGill University. She taught for twenty years at McGill, Concordia University and John Abbott College. She lives in Montreal.